Acknowled

With thanks to Margaretha Mont... ... .gg..... .. it, calmed my anxieties and helped with the publication of this book. Thank you to my fellow Word Weavers who inspired me to write.

Thanks also to Rosie McCall for her fiendishly fun writing exercises and to my family and friends who have been so encouraging and helpful in providing feedback on my stories.

Biggest thanks of all to Andrea Byrne, life-long muse, laugh maker, artist and parfumier extraordinaire.

Cover, 'The Ace of Cups' by Andrea Byrne

This collection of short stories is entirely a work of fiction.

The names, characters and incidents portrayed in it are the work of the author's imagination. Any resemblance to actual persons, living or dead, events or localities is entirely coincidental.

No AI was used in this book.

Introduction

The stories in this book are a whimsical mix inspired by chance encounters, bits and pieces overheard and snippets from the hand me down tapestry of family stories. I am constantly surprised at where a story notion leads. I have read that many writers have a specific room devoted to their work. This helps with concentration, consistency and flow. I don't, as illustrated by the longest story in the book, which is lurking at the back and has several moods filtering in from where I happened to be staying at the time. Writing is a craft. I'm still learning. It's what I love. I write with the reader in mind. My aim is to amuse, to communicate and touch a chord. Some of the content may be considered a little risqué. The intention is not to shock and certainly not to offend, but to enhance the story. I hope you like the characters and enjoy the stories.

The Stories

Drifting By	……	5
The Listening Pines	……	22
Maria's Mask	……	30
Summer Pastures	……	55
The Fish Dinner	……	68
Lifecycles	……	71
Darkness and Bright	……	81
The Love of Mothers	……	107
Ace of Cups – A Christmas Tale	……	117
The Food of Love	……	129
To Leave The Cupboard	……	141

Drifting By

Smoke! I turned to Bryony, crouched on the sand, filling her pockets with shells.

"Come on!" I said, "Let's go see who's living in Drifting By."

"What?" She turned to me, annoyed by the interruption, blue eyes like mine, but flinty not spaced-out looking.

"The house by the slipway."

Her frown followed my point.

"There's someone living in it. See the smoke coming out the chimney?"

She sighed and went back to shells.

"Come on," I said, "I'll race you to the mermaid's rock. I'll count twenty, give you a head start."

She stood up, pocketing her treasures, giving me a steady look. "Really twenty Mummy. No cheating!"

"Really twenty," I promised and off she went, determined to win, wellies fast smacking the wet sand.

"Nineteen, Twenty. I'm coming Bryony Gavey." I screamed.

She screamed too and ran faster. I let her win and we sat on rocks, catching breath. She was staring at the cottage with its whisps of smoke, wind salt tears magnifying her eyes.

"Is that why its called Drifting By?" she asked.

Instantly images of drift-wood shelves, lop-sided cupboards and weird sculptures pictured my mind; scents from huge vases overflowing with flowers, coffee from a growling, hissing machine and joss-sticks stuck about the place; licking big slabs of dripping raspberry ripple ice-cream jammed between wafers; murmurings, laughter, shouting and slamming of doors; memories walloped me like a big screen film with extra sensorial effects.

"Mum!" Bryony was looking at me in that scrutinizing way she has. "Who used to live there?"

Suddenly, I was at a loss, couldn't care less, "I'm a bit cold now," I said "Let's go home. We'll go see another day."

"Can we walk along the giant's fingertips?" She was already heading towards them, my girl always determined.

We stepped on the first lumps of two lines of wood poking out of the sand. Ten giant fingertips. It was him who'd first called them that. Him with the arty father and glamorous mother, him with the flinty, blue eyes. Michael.

I watched Bryony jump from one 'fingertip' trying to reach the next and thought of other legs making the leap. Two sets of brown, almost reaching, my brothers' and another paler set, Michael's. All in bathing trunks, the sun always shining. Then the dash for the ladder set into the high sea wall, me screaming "Wait!", them racing up then leaning over the wall shouting, "Too slow Nancy!" "Slow coach!" "Hurry up Nance or we'll go without you!"

While I panted over the hot, dry sand, they'd fling seagull discarded limpet shells at my head, chanting in unison the theme tune from 'The Bionic Man', 'Nah nah nah naah naah'.

As Bryony and I walked up the lane, I retold the story of the giant who kept eating children until the islanders hatched a plan to get rid of him. They dug a giant-sized hole in the bay and knitted a child. They threw the wool child in the hole and showed the giant. When he'd climbed down, all the islanders dug sand into the hole. They trapped him, knees, chest, blood-stained head until only his fingertips were sticking out. His digits wiggled for weeks but after that it was safe for children to jump on them. It made me happy to tell her the story. It was our story, Michael and mine.

I passed the night willing it would be Michael's family staying in Drifting By as they had for so many summers. I dreaded finding others in there now. Summer memories filled my sleepless head. Rock-pooling, bombshells off the wall at high tide, blissful, endless mooching. He'd seemed a lonely weirdo at first, trailing behind his flowing haired, flower-power mother. They both had long legs and a loping sort of walk. The antelopes, that's what we called them.

"Go on Michael. Go and make friends!" We heard her tell him, a classy voice from under the big orange hat and dark sunglasses.

Michael started hanging around, but Steve and Rodney took offence and gave him a hiding. I hated them for that, shouted and screamed and jumped on their backs. Up on the slipway, Mick the Fish put down the nets he was mending and came striding towards us. "Oi! Cut that out!" and we all ran. The pecking order established, we became a foursome, each summer growing taller, exploring further, competing harder until Steve then Rodney got jobs and motorbikes, then it was just Michael and me.

Sometimes we went to each other's. Michael preferred coming to ours. I preferred his. Their cottage was a bazaar, it even had a telescope and Michael's parents were like a theatre show. Unused to displays of adult affection, at first I was embarrassed by Yvonne and Robert's smoochy kisses, always initiated by Yvonne.

"Kiss, I need a kiss," she would say and he would sigh and deliberately stop whatever he was doing, like she was a pain but then he'd smile into her eyes, giving a little shake of his head before putting his lips to hers. I would look away, discomforted and piqued by a weird sort of envy.

Yvonne friendly as a girl, a bikini sporting, bracelet clinking film star of a mother. Always Martinis or Cinzanos swirling in chunky glasses. She treated us like adults and talked about things my parents would never speak of. Things I doubted they even knew about. By contrast, dark, unruly haired Robert was taciturn, intense as the smell of the whisky in the glass he so often charged with a quick shoot of soda from the shiny red or green syphons. Robert's charm was a rare creature but when he smiled at you, it was the best thing in the world. He smoked strong smelling cigarettes from strange blue packets, French I found out later, sending smoke curling around the room and he was always covered in paint or plaster or sparks, rarely paying Yvonne the attention she felt she deserved. So we became her diversions. Michael seemed embarrassed by her but I felt flattered that she wanted to talk to me.

"Oh! Saucy Nancy!" Yvonne purred when she found out my name. She held my chin in her hand, floral perfume wafting up my nostrils, her skin so smooth, even her lipstick smelt nice. "We're going to have to watch you with our boy, aren't we!"

Innocent and uncertain, I smiled and saw my silly face reflected in huge sunglasses. Robert tutted.

"We're going to explore the pine forest," Michael blurted, "Come on let's go."

"Off you go then," Yvonne released me with a starlet smile and I turned from her to follow Michael, already outside and running up the path.

The cottage was dismally empty for most of the time. Every year they would arrive in the big car with the fairy on the bonnet two weeks before my school broke up for summer. Yvonne also had a Beetle convertible which she kept at the cottage. Every week she sped off to town on the other side of the island and would return with carloads of treasures.

"What now?" Robert would sneer as a fluffy pouffe or a new bag emerged from a posh shop carrier bag and she would make faces at him, take bags upstairs and we'd hear her thumping around on the wooden floor. A little later she'd come down in a dress of crocheted cream or brightly coloured fabric that smelt of India.

"You look beautiful," I'd breathe awestruck, but her husband and son refused to even notice. I couldn't understand it any more than I could understand Yvonne's frequent and sustained campaigns of digs at Robert which resulted in some truly spectacular rows. The first time I witnessed one I was terrified.

"Are they ok?" I asked, wondering who to call for help, as we retreated to the beach.

"They'll be fine," Michael said dismissively, "They're like that all the time."

But sometimes, Yvonne's sunshades hid black eyes and once my shocked eyes clocked that Robert had one. Other times when we crept in, there would be loud, creaking from the telescope room, at which Michael would quickly grab change from a jar and take me to the beach café instead.

My home was so boring in comparison. Mum and Dad in their overalls, working away in the tomato ripening greenhouses, potato or flower fields or off delivering in the big grey truck that chuffed out black smoke and the house so sparse and dull. Michael said that he loved the order and calm. He even liked helping Dad, not like us lot who were always finding excuses not to. They chatted away about crop prices and pests and the mystifying decisions of the Tomato Board. I thought he was being ultra polite but Michael said he enjoyed Dad's company, found him interesting. He even said he liked the hot, green smell of tomatoes. Mum and Dad thought the world of him of course but he was my friend and wanting him to myself I would prise him away from them at the first opportunity.

Once after a long swim trying to chase a seal, we were resting on the shingle bank. He must have been fifteen that year, me fourteen. I was flat out on the hot shingle and Michael was sitting leaning against a rock, staring out to the light house and glittering sea.

"Your parents are so decent," said Michael out of nowhere. He almost sounded envious.

"Yours are so exotic," I countered, pleased with finding that word, "Fancy having a film star mother and artist father. Much more interesting than boring old growers. I can't believe I've even met them."

"They're fakes," he said.

I shielded my eyes with my hand so I could look at him.

His face was set hard, "Just fakes." He looked down picked up a small ormer shell, absently wiping shingle out of it with his thumb, exposing the smooth mother of pearl within.

"Mum had a small part in a rubbish film years ago and Dad's 'art' is just a waste of space and a waste of an awful lot of money. They're fakes and they know it. That's why they drink so much."

I sat up, the celebrity nights and posh galleries fragmenting in my mind. I'd never heard Michael sound so bitter.

"But where do they get their money from then?" I asked, almost not believing.

Michael flicked the shell away, started fiddling with some dried seaweed stuck to a mermaid's pouch.

"My grandfather, that's who," He glanced at me, "Grandfather, now he was a success. He was a composer, very famous, Gerald Hanover. He did a lot of film scores."

I was ashamed to admit that I hadn't heard of him or even one of the famous films Michael listed.

"Doesn't matter, not your thing, but the point is he made the money and those two are like spoilt kids getting their way all the time even though nothing ever really makes them happy. My mother can't stop buying stuff, and not just little stuff, there's the French chateau, the Swiss ski resort, she bought those for him as birthday presents for God's sake. We never even go there! Fancy cars; every time I go home there's a new kitchen or a pool-side bar or carpets again. It's crazy. This place was another birthday present." He shook his head and I felt hurt.

"At least we come here," he added then smiled at me, "And I'm glad we do."

"Me too," I told him and flopped back down. In my relief I writhed around in the dry shingle which stuck to my still damp skin. Thinking about what he'd said I turned over, covering my front and arms and legs too. To cheer him up I stood up, showed off my state.

"Like my suit?" I asked and he laughed and did the same then we walked up the beach like two seaside ghosts, laughing again as some kids with their mums pointed at us.

Michael and I, it seemed that something precious was sealed between us after that day. I began seeing his parents in a new light. Over the next two summers, our eyes often met in understanding at things his mother did and said and those his father didn't. I also came to be a bit more appreciative of my more ordinary but solid mum and dad.

That last summer, Michael was working out what he would do now school was over. His exam results were brilliant, I was just hoping to have done well enough to stay on to do mine. We still had mad moments, but impending adulthood made us more thoughtful, well him anyway. In between the old fun and the new talking, a lot of flaunting and furtive glancing was going on. His last afternoon, we found ourselves in the old smugglers' cave. He told me that he didn't want to leave, and I didn't want him to go. We started kissing. We started exploring. We couldn't stop and there's not much to stop you if you're only wearing swimmers and a bikini. So many memories, and so many times since have I asked myself, why he never came back.

Next day was sunny. I took Bryony and lunch to the beach. We swam and munched. I kept squinting towards Drifting By but it was too hazy to make out anything. By about four we were walking up the slip that took us to the cottage. My heart was beating so loud, I was surprised Bryony didn't ask what the noise was.

"Go pull that string," I told her and she skipped up the path and clanged the bell. The shell wind chimes made their tinkling sing-song and she turned and grinned at me, eyes a-sparkle. I was holding my breath. The door creaked open and then, heart slam, Michael. He looked a bit that way too, especially when he noticed Bryony smiling up at him. Another head poked out, and he introduced us to Corinne. I managed a smile and Corinne invited us to tea in the garden. Walking through the house, Bryony gazed about as I had once done. Corinne was pretty with chestnut hair in a shiny bob. My salt-bleached halo didn't compare well. She was full of how lovely it was to meet me. Thankfully Bryony took over,

"I love Drifting By," she told them, "Please can I see the telescope?"

"I'll show you," Michael said and took her hand. I trailed behind, a lump in my throat, my dream gone wrong.

She was thrilled by the telescope, "I can see lots of blue," she confirmed, peering through, hand over one eye.

Michael laughed. "Its better at night" he told her, "We'll have to come back in winter."

'We' clanged, twisting my guts.

Corinne called. Back in the garden. I asked Michael about Yvonne and Robert. Corinne gave a start.

"They're dead." he said and I stared at him in shock.

I had shown Bryony photos of them inside. She was looking at Michael. "Why did they die?" she asked.

Michael looked at me. "Robert died of…depression," he took in Bryony and left it at that. "Mother died in a skiing accident shortly before."

I could picture the row that had led to her decision to go.

"I'm so sorry." Useless words.

Bryony did what I wanted to do. She got up on to Michal's lap and put her arms around him, laid her head on one of his shoulders, while patting the other. Then she sighed, got down and went back to her chair.

"Cherry or chocolate?" Corinne asked, offering plates of sliced cake.

"There was a lot to sort out," Michael said flatly, cake in front of him. "Then I got a job. It helped."

"In Commodities and doing very well." Corinne said, pouring more tea in my cup. "That's where we met. I'm a P.A. at the same firm."

"What's a Pee A.?" Bryony asked.

"Its someone who does all the work for someone else and doesn't get paid nearly as much." Michael told her.

Corinne laughed, shaking her head. "What about you Nancy?"

I worked at the co-op up the road.

"Mummy's the youngest supervisor on the island." Bryony told them.

"Fame at last!" I said feebly.

Corinne smiled, "And what about your husband?"

"Oh, I haven't got one of those."

Why did I come here?

"I've got a rabbit called Daisy, she's brown and a cat called Fanny, she's grey and quite naughty." Bryony told them. Bless my child.

Michael's penetrating eyes were on me. "And where are you living?"

I had to admit that we lived with my parents.

He nodded. Those blue eyes. Then he said, "Say hello to everyone from me."

"Yes of course." I shot up. "Well, we'd better love you and leave you. Come on Bryony, time to go."

The poor little thing quickly shoved the last of her cake in and stood up. We said goodbyes and that we were sure to see each other. *Not likely!*

Bryony was full of it when we got back. Mum hid her own disappointment, Dad too, nothing was said. My poor parents. The growing business they'd worked so hard to build with an eye on buying old Tosty's land when he gave up would never turn into Gavey Brothers Limited. Steve and Rodney had worked hard - good, saved up - good, sold Suzukis and gone to Australia - bad, and their daughter had got pregnant with no father in sight at seventeen – very bad. It had been hard that first year of Bryony. I loved her of course but I shed a lot of tears. Mum and Dad were amazing. As well as being the best grandparents ever, they got me through it, made me pull myself together. One day they sat me down, told me to get any job for now.

"You can't be this house bound Love," Mum said, "Once she's at school Nancy, you'll go to night school and get your A levels. With Bryony here you'll find the time passes ever so fast, it'll be here before you know it."

"You're still young Nance," Dad added, somehow still proud, "You've got a great future ahead of you."

He hugged me and my tears dribbled into his shirt. What would I have done without them?

My flat deposit shrank over the next week, but it was nice watching Bryony at the zoo and the fair and the new trampoline place. We didn't see Michael and Corinne. Not till the Monday. They were leaving, heading to the port. I was back to work and followed them up the hill, them in their shiny car, me in my wreck. Holiday over, back to sugar spills in Aisle 3. People were pleased to see me, which was nice except for purvey Aidan. Hope was over too, my Michael dream just a splattered sandcastle.

Next day, Mum took Bryony to town. When I got in, she showed me her new school dress and shoes. I let her think I was thrilled but I was worried for her, the fatherless child and sad for me. I didn't want my little girl growing up and away from me. She was all I was ever going to have.

"There's a letter for you," Mum said.

I was hoping for a letter from Rodney or Steve with photos of koalas and wombats for Bryony.

Bryony skipped to the dresser and danced over to me with the envelope, white, official looking but delivery with a smile.

"Thank you, Ma'am." I said and off she skipped, singing away.

I turned the envelope over. Heart thud. I recognised that writing.

Michael!

The Listening Pines

Ssshh! We're listening. We like to know what's going on. Ssshh! Here we stand on our hill. Glossy, green needles brush the summer sky. Our hill goes steeply down to rock and pebbles, sand and sea. The wind battered earth is held in place by our roots. People trip and sometimes we murmur our quiet amusement at their tumble. Not always. Here we thrash in the gales and whisper in the breeze and we listen. We hear everything. We always know! Ssshh! Quieten down! I'm trying to listen.

Here's a hefty tread, though muffled by discarded needles. The man who walks early with his big, young dog. We hear it thundering around. The dog runs everywhere, down to the sea and up again, effortless and boundless in its enthusiasm to explore. It only stops for a massive shake. It shakes the sea from its furry head to the feathers of its tail. The man plods. He is heavy. He whistles to let his dog know where to find him. He laughs at the happy, shiny creature as it hurtles towards him, only to dash off again. They pass below our burdened branches. They weave through our black, grooved trunks then the pounding recedes. They are returning home. A man has to work, but they'll be back.

Ssshh! What's happening? What do you hear? Ssshh! I will tell you.

A softer foot fall. Ah yes. We know. This is the careful walk of the old man and his old dog. This man worries he will slip and slide on our orange carpet. Even soft cushions shock old bones. Thud of stick as he jams it in to stop himself falling. Slow, old man talks to his gentle, old friend. They grunt and pant as they struggle up and down the slopes. Pass it on, it's the old man. Tell the others. The old dears are passing through.

Now it's just us and the birds. Our songbirds and the big, white seabirds, screaming of their news.

"Fishing boat heading out."

The sun arcs its daily journey over us. Our branches sway, we hush ourselves a lullaby.

Lots of steps, running light. It's the children. The children are here.

"Be careful!" shout the mothers.

We listen but the children don't.

"Is it here? Can we reach it today?" they shout, rushing to be first.

The rope is down, not confiscated by the mean winds. The rope tied by the older children to one sturdy bough creaks under their delighted weights. They swing out in a circle of orange, out towards the shimmering sea. Out and round and back again. We hear their shrieks of joy and cries of "My turn, my turn. Get off!"

The mothers and the smallest child collect our cones. We hear the bag rustle as another one goes in.

Blonde lady says to blonde child, "Well done Toby, that was a big one."

He beams at her. He's happy because his best person has noticed his good find. She smiles at him. He is her treasure. The mothers don't stop talking. They talk of other people. What this person said, what that person did. We are party to their conversation. We know and what we know, we pass on. All the trees are whispering. The bag is full of big, dry cones now. The mothers call the other children to them.

"Come along. Time to go. Time for tea."

The rope queue pretends not to hear at first. They don't want to leave but then they run to follow.

"Wait!" shouts the youngest, always last and left suspended in mid-air, "Wait for me!"

He scuffles to get himself landed and runs to catch up, "Wait!"

Happy voices get quieter and little figures get smaller. We hear goodbyes, doors slam and cars drive away.

The sun is over the lighthouse now. We hear a steady phut, phut, phut. The boat and the gulls are returning.

"Good catch, good catch," squeal the gulls.

Gentle winds caress us, wafting our perfume along the shingly shoreline. The tide is low. Our scent mingles with the sun-dried seaweed, the gorse on the headland and the salt smell of the sea.

Crack of twig. Ssshh! What's that? Who's there? Sure footsteps. Is it her? Oh yes, it is! It's the woman. What's she wearing? The green dress with the buttons. She's waiting for the man to come to her. She leans against a blackened trunk in the den we make for them. She's hoping for an assignation. Ssshh! Listen hard! Is he coming? Can you hear? Yes, yes, pass it on. Pass it on. He's on his way. I hear him coming up the path with the old, stone steps. These two like our secret places for their trysts.

Sneaky feet! Sneaky feet are coming. The peeper minces along the rabbit path. The lovers never hear him, but we do. We know he's there.

The wanted man comes up the tree root path now, running and walking, he doesn't want to get too hot. He enters our needle cave, relieved to see she's there. Sultry eyes meet. They hold each other's gaze. He walks slowly, deliberately to her. The breeze ceases for us to hear their louder heartbeats. We hear him swallow hard. She takes a deep breath. It fills out the curves of the buttoned dress. He's there. His hands reach for and gently cup her face. We hear their long kiss. We hear her moan as buttons are undone. How tantalising. They are ecstatic, these two. His hand runs up her thigh. Her skirt rises with his hand. We hear them. We hear everything.

But ssshh! Listen! What's this? Is that another? Do you hear hesitant following footsteps? Yes, yes, we hear them too. Pass it on. Tell the others. He's been followed. Another lady, the blonde lady is on her way.

What's that?

Another lady's coming. Tell the others. Another lady is coming! The blonde mother. Pale. She has red eyes and a red nose and a scrunched-up handkerchief.

Is she near? Does she know where to look?

Ssshh! What's happening? Tell us.

A sharp intake of breath. The handkerchief presses to her mouth as her eyes take in the truth. Then another deep breath.

"How could you?" Her voice is pain and rage.

The man turns. His face is guilt.

Panicking fingers of the other lady fumble to do up the green buttons. Her heart is pounding even louder but slower, now it pounds with dread and shame.

Hot tears spring from the eyes of the cheated lady. They make her voice a powerful waterfall.

"You are so disgusting," she tells him.

"And you!" Turning, her livid eyes feast on those of our green dressed lady.

"How could you do this to me?" Her voice rises to unleash her fury, "How could you betray me like this?"

The lovers gaze at her. They are struck dumb.

Their dumbness is too much for her to bear.

Her body bends under the force of her anger. "I hate you!" She roars like the sea in a tempest. "I hate you both!"

The whole forest is silenced.

She turns and stomps out of the den. Not far away, she stops and leans against a trusty trunk. Tears run down its furrowed bark.

The statues that were lovers mobilise. He sighs a sad sigh. He turns to follow the departed woman. Then back. He puts hands on the green clad shoulders. He is fervent.

"I'll call you."

She nods. Remorseful. Not sultry now and watches him trudge away from her.

She sits on a fallen trunk. We listen with her.

Accusations scream, outraged threats follow. The betrayed lady's treasures just became her weapons. The man has been found guilty and is helpless in his thwarted bliss. He has no riposte other than. "I'm sorry Mary. I never wanted to hurt you."

To his outraged wife, he may as well be waving a red rag. The green dressed woman hangs her head in her hands. She groans. It is a groan of self-loathing. Suddenly she's up. She runs down the hill. It's too steep for her and she has to clutch at a branch to catch up with her legs. The branch rips through the delicate skin of her arm. She's doing a big circle around the embattled couple. She reaches the road that hugs the bay and we hear her sandals as she runs and runs. She wants to drive away before those other two come near. She makes her escape just in time. The shaky couple enter the carpark as her car disappears. These two have run out of words. They drive away in their separate cars.

Sneaky peeper is disappointed. He goes and touches the tree where the green dress leaned. He sniffs it but bark is bark. For once, he uses the main path. No need for sneaking now. As the last car drives away, the forest noises resume. The birds sing good evening. The crickets sing that the night is yet young. The red, gold sun slides below the circle of sea. Pink, gold sky turns grey to blue black. It's owl time. She announces her hunt. Stars glitter in sky and sea. The moon swings by. We whisper amongst ourselves. Ssshh… We whisper of what we've heard and learned. Ssshh… We're always whispering amongst ourselves and remember this, we're always listening.

Maria's Mask

Maria was Harlequin. Of all the roles in the fantastical family that made up the Italian Comedy, his was hers. Harlequin's quizzical mask and diamond pattern were the costume she had been born for, certainly raised for. Maria was the image of her father, Alberto Buongiorno, in dark-eyed looks and stature and shared his indomitable magnetism. She was graced with the same cat sure body, honed to express all the moods, contradictions and flagrant absurdities of Harlequin's personality and it was Maria, not her brothers who had been the chosen one.

Had been. For Alberto had changed his mind. She was watching him now, her eyes and mouth set hard as he trained her replacement. Roberto would never make as good a Harlequin. Too tall for a start, too rigid. Although under Alberto's rigorous priming, she had to admit Roberto was getting better. And of course, Harlequin could be any height. Maria stared at her father, insolent and wrathful. How could he do this to her?

Maria and her older brothers, Alessandro and Roberto had grown up watching and learning the various roles and scenarios of the Commedia dell' Arte. They had become adept and could slip into any role, exchanging with uncles and cousins, subordinating their own personality into that of the character they were playing at the time. Alberto was a famous Harlequin and all three of his elder children were learning everything they could of his craft, aping his every move - and who wouldn't? But the boys lacked the dexterity, the necessary flip from crazy trick to reflection mid-air in high somersault that only father and daughter possessed. Maria had always taken it for granted that her brothers would take on the roles of the preying knave, Brighella, the avaricious merchant, Pantaloon, the charlatan Doctor, boastful Captain and any other characters, bears or ostriches. These roles were essential to the show, and exciting in their way but Harlequin, the rubber-bodied prince of Zannis was the best and the most demanding.

Amongst the Buongiorno family troupe, Alberto's strong constitution was a legend. There was only one occasion when he had been indisposed due to illness and it had been Maria who Alberto had called to stand in for him. At the age of just twelve. In Venice! The crowd had been large and boisterous. Such entertainments in the 17th century were an imperative to make time and head to the square. As she had done so many times, Maria relived watching intently, waiting for her first public entrance as Harlequin.

The audience murmur and bump shoulders as the parting curtain reveals a flower garden with a mermaid sitting on the edge of a pool. The mermaid, (Maria's aunt) *creates a fountain by filling and emptying a small watering can. The mermaid's face is a study of grace.*

A beautiful lady (Maria's mother) *stands near the pool.*

Harlequin somersaults on to the stage and loiters, gazing at the lady through the small eye holes of his black facemask. From his stance the audience know that this lady, the lady Rosaria is his beloved, his 'inamorata'.

Rosaria is looking around, searching for someone else. Harlequin picks imaginary flowers and gives them to Rosaria. She sniffs the blooms, nods her thank you then resumes her searching.

Seeking inspiration on how to impress, Harlequin cups his hand to his ear – birdsong! Looking up he spies an ornate birdcage. He glances furtively around then deftly unhooks the cage and peeks in. Harlequin begs the bird to sing a beautiful song so that Rosaria will fall in love with him. He nods, sharing his delight with the audience. The bird has agreed. Harlequin presents the birdcage to Rosaria, swaying from side to side in front of her, hoping she will bestow a smile on him or maybe even a kiss. Rosaria accepts his gift but barely notices for she is in love with Brighella.

The audience knows that scoundrel Brighella is only interested in her so he can steal the valuables of her father, the rich merchant, Pantaloon. Brighella slopes onto the stage. The slant-almond eyes of his green mask, with its hooked nose and twirling moustache leave little doubt, the swaggering walk and unscrupulous gaze confirm – this man is a rogue. Today, he is a charming rogue as he catches Rosaria's eye, beckons her to him and they dance.

Heartbroken, Harlequin crouches, weeping so many silent tears that he has to keep wringing out the cloth he uses to wipe them. Full of concern, the 'soubrette' maid, Columbine (Maria's older sister) comes to his side. He mimes slashing his wrists, plunging a knife into his stomach, hanging himself. Wide-eyed Columbine is at a loss, then decides what she must do. She brings him a chamber pot full of tagliatelle. Harlequin eats and eats. As he eats, Maria pulls material from a concealed bag and stuffs it in Harlequin's shirt. *Columbine watches, sharing her anxiety with the crowd, as Harlequin's stomach grows bigger and bigger.*

Harlequin becomes ill and clutches his swollen stomach, writhing and grimacing, pulling on Columbine's dress, beseeching her to save him. Columbine calls to Rosaria and Brighella, telling them to fetch the doctor. The black-frocked, red-cheeked doctor arrives and prescribes an enema, brandishing from his bag a comedically large enema dispenser. Despite his pains, Harlequin stands, shaking his head in exaggerated refusal then leaps from the stage. Out of sight Maria takes a huge swig of water. *The ladies persuade Harlequin to come back. The doctor and Brighella persuade him to bend over. The ladies turn daintily away.*

There are hoots and shrieks of laughter, lewd and shocked from the audience and bawdy shouts of encouragement. As the doctor administers the enema, Harlequin spouts water from his mouth into the mermaid's pool. The mermaid is aghast at this insulting intrusion of her domain.

Two frill-necked bears clamber onto the stage and frighten everyone away except the fountain tipping mermaid. Her grace of face has been restored. Harlequin bounces back, somersaults over the surprised bears who begin to dance. Harlequin waltzes around them. The bears follow him as he walks on his hands and then tumbling in the air leads them off the stage.

Hats had flown to shouts of 'Bravo!' and 'Encore!' And that had been just the first scene. It had been the best day of Maria's life. She had performed every trick, every turn and gesture just as she had been taught. Flouting her father's instruction not to, and to the delight of the crowd, she had spiced up the scenarios by improvising the discourse. After all, that was the point of the Commedia dell' Arte. The eyes of the other characters had glinted with amusement and the improvisation had taken flight. Her timing and tomfoolery were as impeccable as they felt natural. The admiring reaction of the audience and the rest of the troupe had confirmed the matter. Maria was Harlequin.

Except that now, she wasn't.

Maria's mother, Flavia had tried to warn her.

"Harlequin is a role for men," Flavia had said, "He's too rude for us ladies."

"Then I will be a most genteel Harlequin," Maria had answered with a gallant bow.

One day, when Maria was practising somersaulting from the raised stage to the grass below, Flavia came and presented her with a fluttery dress.

Maria stared at the dress in bewilderment, ignoring the approving comments of Roberto and Alessandro.

"Come and learn to dance and sing with Valentina and Aunt Silvia." Flavia had coaxed in her beautiful voice. "The feminine roles are fun too and not as easy as they look."

Maria had stretched out her arms in comic questioning, "Why?"

"Come and try. For me?"

"Tomorrow. Maybe tomorrow." Maria had smiled before scaling the ladder and launching herself into a perfect double somersault.

Alberto had been standing right there, but he could choose to be deaf and blind sometimes.

When Maria was thirteen, a game of kiss-chase at a lively fair, led to a life changing event. It was almost eight months later that Flavia pointed to and felt Maria's still only slightly distended belly and told her daughter that the air tumbling was going to have to stop as she was most certainly far gone with child. Father and daughter were incredulous, but Flavia was right. The tiny baby, snugly curled, was soon ready to be born. Maria's fit young body delivered her baby boy, with its usual efficiency. Maria in her youth and singlemindedness considered baby Federico more as she would a sibling. In her mind, nothing had changed. The day after he was born, she left him fed and snug with Flavia and shocked as her body might be, headed to Alberto for daily practise.

Alberto watched Maria's approach. Roberto and Alessandro were with him, eyes averted.

"What are you doing here?" Alberto snapped.

Maria sought the special look he had always bestowed on her. She stretched her arms to her sides, hands upwards, waggling her body, "Training of course."

"No Maria," Alberto snapped, his widespread hands went up in negation, "that is finished. Mamma will teach you the feminine roles now."

He turned his back on her. Disbelieving Maria caught his arm.

"No!" Her heart was pounding, blood rushing, "I'm still Harlequin."

Strong hands grasped her shoulders, turned and led her away. He spun her to face him, furious eyes holding hers.

"This has to stop. You are a woman, Maria." Eyes stone hard, "Roberto is Harlequin. Not you."

"Take her!" He barked at Flavia, who had followed Maria and she and Valentina led a reeling Maria away.

Maria mourned for Harlequin. She fed baby Federico and he thrived but she didn't find the joy in him that she knew was expected. If it wasn't for him, she'd be out with her father and brothers. Flavia, Aunt Silvia and Maria's older sister, Valentina fluttered around cooing at the baby and coaxing smiles from him. They did everything they could to pique Maria's interest in the lively wit of the soubrettes, cantarinas, ballerinas and lovers. Maria stared glumly out at them. Her younger sister and cousins were already little ladies. Not Maria, she hated the fussiness of femininity. Pretending to be a statue that suddenly moved – how dull, or a naughty soubrette, dancing nymphs or worst of all a lover.

Maria knew Valentina struggled to understand her, but her sisterly love was evident,

"You can be Columbine, Maria," she offered, "We can share the role."

Columbine was Harlequin's special friend and the most arch of the female roles.

Maria was touched by so generous an offer, hugged Valentina but shook her head, "How can I take your role when I don't even want it?"

Valentina hugged Maria back, not quite hiding her relief.

The constant need for new scenarios kept the ladies busy. Histories, fables and sonnets were studied and mined for ideas. For Maria, they doubled their efforts, trying to entice her interest.

Olivette, a servant girl has a child by Brighella, who she had believed to be in love with her. Brighella disappeared as soon as he discovered the pregnancy. Olivette's friend, Columbine tries to help her. Columbine asks her mistress, Rosaria if Olivette and the baby can come and live with them at the house of Pantaloon. Rosaria agrees.

Unaware of this development, Brighella now sets his eye on Columbine and follows her into the garden. Olivette sees and tells Rosaria who sends for the Captain. Olivette goes to hang out the washing, very slowly. Brighella watches her, annoyed that his sweet nothings must wait for her to go back inside. He bides his time, strumming on his lute, encouraged to note that Columbine's hands are clasped in appreciation.

The Captain has had previous dealings with this vagabond Brighella and surprises the would-be lover by rushing into the garden, shouting and brandishing his sword. Cowardly Brighella runs to Olivette and hides under her overturned wash basket. Olivette sits on the wash basket, followed by Rosaria and then Columbine.

"This seat is warm, is it not?" they cry, hiding their amusement.

The Captain rushes around, thrashing his sword for the benefit of the ladies and bellowing for Brighella to show himself. The ladies deny all knowledge so he decides that the scoundrel must have gone to the port and dashes after him. The ladies stand but Brighella is wedged into the laundry basket. They call him their pet tortoise and try to coax his head out of its shell by offering him fruit. Brighella scowls at the audience then makes his escape, crawling away in humiliation.

Maria was unimpressed. She didn't participate in the excitable exchanges of ideas.

Somewhat offended by her daughter's bored face, Flavia pointed out,

"If it's improvisation that you want Maria, this is it."

Maria disagreed. However, she jumped at the chance when Uncle Nico offered to teach her to walk the tightrope. and was soon not merely walking but jumping high and landing on the rope. This was better! Until she found out that she had to do it in a dress. The overtight bodice constricted her breathing and the flapping of the admittedly light and shortened dress finished that idea. Poor Aunt Silvia's suggestion that they create a scenario especially for Maria with Harlequin met with uncontrolled rage.

Flavia wouldn't give up. "Maria, everyone can sing, just as everyone can dance." she insisted when Maria refused to even try.

Maria tried but Flavia's optimism was ill-founded. Maria shared her father's squeaky voice, so perfect for delivering Harlequin's quips and philosophies but hardly suitable for 'La Bella Cantarina'. Watching her mother and aunt trying to look as if they were enjoying her recital while Valentina accompanied her so prettily on the viol resulted in another fit of anger.

"Not everyone!" Maria hissed, tears of humiliation spilling as she wrenched off her dress and marched away. On her own, in her underclothes she went back to somersaults and scenarios for one.

Whilst part of Maria knew Alberto would never allow her to play Harlequin again, her will refused to accept it. She became nothing. For years! For nothing, her will made her continue with the punishing training. Stubborn as her father, she immersed herself in observation of Harlequin. Alberto was the best and Maria watched him all the time but she was also fascinated to observe different interpretations when her family crossed paths with other troupes as they did from time to time. She practised all the gestures, trickeries, and ripostes, becoming a hybrid, becoming perhaps even better than her father.

Federico held a special place in his grandmother's heart. Uncles and aunts made a fuss of him, the younger children amused him, but every child wants the love of his mother, and it was on Maria, that his gaze would always settle. Wherever she was, Federico tried to follow.

Maria didn't want him there. "You'll get hurt. Keep out of the way."

Maria ignored him but those dark eyes were always watching her.

When Federico began doing cartwheels and somersaults, Maria had to notice and his huge grin when she praised his efforts was so delightful that Maria felt her rock of a heart suddenly melt.

She pulled him to her, "So Federico, it's you who will be our next Harlequin."

The impish head nodded, silently beaming.

"After me!"

More exaggerated nodding.

Maria became business like, as Alberto had once been with her, "Legs and back are straight for cartwheels, you get your toes right up to that sky. Off you go!"

And off he went, as eager to please as she had once been.

Frustration gnawed, *Ready as I'll ever be, still no role, still no hope of having one.*

They were entering the town of Bergamo, Harlequin's hometown. Maria felt a sudden thrill. A banner was proclaiming that the Buonanotte troupe were also in town. A little later, she slipped away to watch the competition.

The performance was lacklustre in comparison with the last time she'd watched the Buonanotte show. Their new Harlequin was too big, too solid, too slow. Maria looked more closely. Surely that was Gabriele playing Harlequin. Gabriele was also playing Brighella and the Captain. Her heart skipped a beat. He'd noticed her. A game of kiss-chase flashed between them. He blew her a kiss and her answering smile widened in disbelief, was that a blush under Brighella's olive-tinted mask?

As the crowd drifted away, Maria stayed. Gabriele came over to her. Something about his slightly swaggering gait made her heart sing. As was customary, they cheek kissed four times then Maria greeted the rest of the depleted Buonanotte troupe and offered to help pack up.

"Three roles, that's a lot." Maria looked up at Gabriele as they stacked the props under the stage.

Gabriele nodded, "My father died, so I had to take on Harlequin until we can find a replacement." He sighed, "Not easy. Then my uncle died,"

Maria watched him stuff costumes into a bag. Gabriele smiled at her, dashing but still a shyness, "I'm happy to play the Captain, Doctor or even Pantaloon but…"

Maria smiled, "Brighella - that's your role, isn't it?"

Gabriele nodded, puffing his chest up, eyes shining then serious, "And finding a talented Harlequin…" he shook his head, "Impossible."

 A thought struck him, "Unless…"

He looked at Maria and she looked at him. He grinned; she smiled.

Improvisation was the name of their game. They spent the rest of the night as might tomcats parading through town. Brighella and Harlequin, friends and sometime foes since the beginning of time. Theirs was the perennial endeavour to gain the upper hand by quips, tricks, baton or dagger. These two with their distinctive gaits, the sashay and the stut reconquered Bergamo. They sparred under arches, sang from the balconies and charged up steps and down. Whether dancing around fountains, prancing the rooftops or attaining the pinnacle of wit, they surprised each other. All the while, they were developing ideas and gleefully sharing buffoonery and appreciation of each other's talents.

As the bakeries opened, their noses took them into one and they broke the fast together.

Brighella, as the lizard changes from green to brown, became Gabriele, "You'll join us?"

Maria looked into his hopeful eyes.

His gaze held hers, so full of conflicting emotions. Abandoning one's family to join another troupe was a betrayal of love and much more.

The dark eyes steadied, "Yes."

He knew she meant it now but that she might waver.

He grinned and spread his hands before him, "We'll be here til noon."

She kept her eyes on his and nodded.

After the easily conjured magic of the past hours they both knew that if Maria did come, their futures would be made. If she didn't, the only roles she could hope for, were ones she didn't want. And if Gabriele failed to find talented improvisators to replace his father and uncle, the Buonanotte Family troupe would dwindle into oblivion.

Maria's mind was set until her camp came into view. On seeing the familiar homeliness, she suddenly felt exhausted, defeated. Had she really thought she could commit such betrayal? No, she must stay, force herself to settle for the feminine roles.

All those wasted hours of practise.

The hurt she would cause. Her mother, siblings, uncles, aunts. She went through all the beloved faces. They were her family, her security, her life. Love was binding her. Even for Alberto, especially Alberto, even if they barely spoke, even if she hated him.

I have a son!

Flavia and Aunt Daniela were up of course, preparing breakfast for everyone. As usual, Federico was by Flavia's side. He looked at Maria with huge, solemn eyes.

Flavia kissed Maria, then Federico came to greet her.

As was only right, Maria was being sucked back into the Buongiorno fold. Sighing, she smiled wanly at Federico and wrapped her arms around his little body, planting kisses on his cheeks as her mother had just done to her. She knew, for all her motherly faults, she could never leave Federico.

And yet ... yet we were so very good together.

Flavia was watching her, "Did you have a good evening?" she asked with the guileless questioning of her favourite character.

To Maria, it seemed that the recently held conviction of potential meeting success, was capering wildly away.

She caught sight of her father limbering up and Maria knew she was finished here. She stared rooted to the spot.

I must tell him. I can't. I must.

Flavia stood in front of her.

"I hear the Buonanotte family are in need of a new Harlequin."

Flavia's words caught Maria's attention. They shared a look of understanding, sadness, love.

Flavia smiled, tears glistening in her eyes. "I love you very much."

Her voice was strong with emotion, then she nodded in the direction of Alberto and gave Maria a little push,

"You have to do this Maria. You must talk to him. You have to tell him. It has to be you."

Maria felt a simultaneous rush of hope and sickness. She had been expecting remonstrations from her mother, insistence that she stay, not support and encouragement.

Maria nodded. Wise Mamma was right. Heart hammering in dread, she forced her feet to take her over to her father.

"Pappa!"

Alberto turned to Maria in surprise.

Blurting it out was the only way, "The Buonanotte family need a Harlequin so I'm going to them."

Alberto paled, staring at Maria so that she almost buckled under the ferocity of his gaze.

"No!" Alberto's voice was controlled but only just, "I forbid it."

"Why Pappa?" It came out with a sob.

"You would go with the competition when you are needed here with us, with your family?"

"No," Maria shook her head, tears spilling down her cheeks, "I'm not needed here. You know I'm not."

Alberto drew himself up, his face red now, his breathing laboured.

"You are a woman!"

"I am Harlequin. You know that. You're the one who made me!"

Maria thought he would hit her, but his eyes filled, which was worse.

"Get her out of my sight!" he sputtered, spinning on his heel then stalked quickly away.

Flavia led her back to the stove. Maria slumped into a chair. Federico slid onto her lap.

Flavia pulled up a chair and sat too. Silvia put coffee and pastries before them and tactfully withdrew, taking care of the rest of the chores on her own.

Maria looked at her mother, tears distorting her vision, her head leaning on that of Federico. Her heart was tearing in two. Flavia's still brimming eyes took in both her daughter and her grandson.

"I love you both, you know that?"

Maria felt Federico's nod and the bond of love between her mother and son. Flavia was touching both their faces with her infinitely gentle hands.

Then, "Federico," Flavia nodded at him, her voice barely more than a whisper, "It's time for you to fetch our gift."

Federico slid from Maria's knees, opened the large wicker basket where Flavia kept her fabrics and returned with some folded material, tied with a silk ribbon. He put the bundle on Maria's lap and went and stood by his grandmother.

Dumbly, Maria looked from the bundle, back at them.

"Look at what we have made for you, Maria."

Disbelieving and heart pounding, Maria pulled the ribbon.

Black diamonds on light, blue background, this costume was perfect for leaping and tumbling.

New leather mask and baton.

Black toc hat with a feather, perfect for waving and bowing.

"But, you really think I can do this?"

Tears were running down Maria's cheeks and starting to plop onto the material.

Federico hastily retrieved the gift and Flavia folded and re-secured it with the ribbon.

"But," Maria shook her head, then nodding in her father's direction, "I don't think I can."

"You must!" Flavia stood briskly, "Of course he's upset. We will all miss you, don't think we won't but you will go and we will see you again and all will be well."

Hope, disbelief and inconsolable loneliness fought inside Maria's tough, little body.

Flavia held her daughter's shoulders, "Just go! It's kinder." Her voice was firm, then turning again to Federico, "Fetch the bags we put together."

She faced Maria, handing her one of the bags Federico pulled from her basket.

"You will take your son with you. He is adaptable, the next Brighella, Doctor, Harlequin even, Maria, your son can do them all."

Maria glanced from her mother to her son and back to her mother. She was stealing them from each other.

"It won't be easy," Flavia continued, "You'll need to be cook, cleaner and businesswoman as well as tailor. You will need to learn the female roles too. You'll need to be adaptable, diplomatic and all the while creating anew."

She nodded at the bag.

Maria opened it and saw that it contained a comprehensive sewing kit.

"Who else is going to repair your clothes and make new ones? I hear the Buonanotte costumes are looking distinctly shabby."

Tears still sparkling, Maria laughed, tension breaking at last. "That is certainly true."

Then she became pensive. She crouched in front of Federico. "Are you sure you want to come?"

She felt she must stay if he shook his head but no, dark, almost black eyes held hers and he nodded, his small, rounded chin jutting determinedly.

"I'm coming Mamma," he said in his firm but squeaky voice.

"It's both your destinies," Flavia said, "Now, go!"

Maria wept as they left the camp. So much love, so much unsaid, so much unknown, but it was an enormous comfort having Federico walking beside her.

As they approached the Buonanotte camp, Maria's spirits began to lift. Gabriele was on the lookout and visibly delighted to see her. He lifted his arms in welcome and taking in Federico, opened his arms even wider, his eyes questioning how her departure had gone.

Maria, dropped her bags, curled in on herself and bunched her fists turning them in front of her eyes, Harlequin's way of crying.

Gabriele, now Brighella leapt forward, brandishing a handkerchief as big as it was invisible. Delicately he dabbed at Maria or Harlequin's tears, but the tears turned into butterflies and soon all three were leaping in the air trying to catch the butterflies in their imaginary nets. Passers-by stopped to watch, smiling.

Then, because Gabriele was the antithesis of his stage character, he lifted Federico onto his shoulders and taking up his bags, led a smiling Maria towards her new family, a roving home and life of perpetual, graciously portrayed craziness.

Summer Pastures

"A touch too much salt in the supreme." Fabien's comment, confidently knowing, as befitting such a connoisseur, was met with polite acknowledgment by the maître d'. His comments always were. Glenda smiled apologetically at the man as she always did and glanced at Fabien's well-fed features. Fabien cocked his head and winked at her while the table was being unobtrusively re-set for the fourth course. Glenda, brain fuzzy even from the optimally served best of wines in the ambience of this top of restaurants, was feeling physically and mentally fed-up. Her attention alighted on each of the diners seated around the starched linen covered table. She touched on conversation randomly, fleeting as the butterfly on the flowers of the terrace she could see through the window. Outside.

What am I doing here? her inner voice softly urged.

Glenda's anxious grey eyes followed the comparisons made. Her head nodded at the dissections of the chef's modus operandi, shook at the little disappointments, and rested still at the exquisiteness of this, the thisness of that. Glenda's gastronomic lexicon was exhausted. She was, she noted, thinner than the others apart from Ralph who smoked his head off in between testily nibbling morsels but whose appreciation of wine was another story. Martina, who she had sought as an ally when she had been introduced as Geoff's new partner was turning into a veritable gastronome. How disappointing. She had clearly done a lot of homework and seemed keen to impress Fabien with her knowledge. Fabien!

Fabien and Glenda met this set of foodies every first Saturday of the month, but every weekend was dedicated to a restaurant of high calibre. Sometimes they drove all morning to meet friends at a celebrated establishment or travelled further still and made a sumptuously dining night of it. If possible, during one of these sojourns, Glenda would slip out, walk a little, see something of the mountain, lake or seaside, sniff the different air, allow herself to be touched by the place. That she found these moments the most enjoyable part of the weekend troubled her.

When Fabien wasn't enjoying culinary miracles, he was in his den, the splendid sauna and jacuzzi cabin which he had had erected in their garden. Especially the jacuzzi in which he would bob about for hours. He read books, food journals mostly and worked whilst watching the large screen he'd installed in there or just gazed vacuously at nothing. Glenda kept her increasingly rare dips to the suggested time limits.

She no longer found the warm jets relaxing or pleasurable but, as that inner voice chastised, *boring, like the meals.*

Fabien, Glenda, and most of their friends worked in the finance industry. They were conscientious, reliable folk, who earned incomes that enabled them to spend their weekends doing the things they liked to do. Kathy, one of Glenda's colleagues had recently joined a walking group and spent her weekends hiking in the mountains.

Glenda gazed longingly at the photos from Kathy's most recent trip. "I'd love to do that," There was yearning in Glenda's voice, as she compared these wonderful vistas with the impending stuffiness of the coming weekend's extravaganza.

"Why don't you come too Glenda?" Kathy asked,

Glenda couldn't see past Fabien's wall of expectation and shook her head. "I don't think I'm fit enough."

"We have beginners coming this weekend so it will be a gentle walk." Kathy's enthusiasm was setting sparks to Glenda's wish. "You know, I walk every lunchtime to keep my fitness up. There are secret steps all around our hilly town, I never knew about. It's interesting and its good training. You're welcome to join me."

Glenda did and loved her new regime.

On Thursday evening, she summoned up the courage to tell Fabien that she would forego lunch this Saturday.

"Don't be silly," he told her dismissively, "It's been booked for ages. You can't not come. It's the best fish restaurant. There's a three-month waiting list to get a reservation. Of course you're coming."

Glenda felt sick. Such a silly, simple thing but it was like kicking out the corner stone of Fabien's wall. She felt inclined to give in, easier to put off Kathy, put off what she wanted to do, rather than have a great, big wall crash down on her. The butterfly she'd noticed fluttered into her consciousness. *Just do it!* her inner voice insisted.

"Not this time thank you Fabien, I choose to walk in the mountains with Kathy." The calm of her outer voice surprised them both.

Fabien's brief glance at her preposterous obstinacy snapped away.

"Fine!"

Taking out his phone, he jabbed at it with a soft, pale finger and then speaking in his charming voice.

"Martina! Hi, Fabien here. If I were to offer you the chance to join me for a delicious lunch at Tresors this Saturday, what would you say?" He was nodding, "Yes Tresors! Great, I'll see you there at noon."

He cast a smug nod at Glenda. "What do you expect?"

"Fair enough." Glenda nodded back, already on her feet, "I'm just going for a walk." Thanking heaven, she was wearing suitable shoes, Glenda headed quickly towards the door.

"Oh, Come on Glenda!" The wall came crashing after her. "Pilates, yoga, what was it? Zumba, now mountain climbing, you're a joke. You'll get left behind. You'll never be able to keep up."

Glenda got out the door and ran and with each long-legged step, she felt a little bit stronger.

Contrary to Fabien's continued sneering, Glenda did keep up. The walk was challenging but the scenery breath-taking, sky so blue against white snow on the further peaks, lakes of blue and green, waterfalls. They wandered through trees of red and gold, through dark, pine paths and on to the more rigorous slopes. No trees now, just scrubby bushes growing out of lumps of granite and loose-stony paths going up and up. Invigorated, Glenda and her fellow walkers pointed and marvelled. Layers were discarded as the heat rose. Huge birds soared on thermals almost close enough to touch. She loved it and she knew, she had to go further, higher, see and learn more. On returning, Fabien saw her enthusiasm and became conciliatory. They agreed that she would alternate, spend one weekend with him and the other with the walking group.

You don't want to though, do you! Glenda shushed her inner voice. Fabien was trying to be reasonable and so should she.

As winter settled in, mountain walks became less frequent but a list of walks for the new season was circulated. Several involved overnight stays in the mountain refuges. Glenda wanted to do them all, trying to decide which to forgo made her miserable.

Determined to keep as fit as possible, Glenda spent as much time as she could walking with Kathy or alone, no matter what the weather was doing. Leaving Fabien to his restaurant guides and steamy bobbing was something of a relief. Glenda also changed her diet, preferring the natural foods, fresh and unfussed, suggested by the group to keep her body fit and ready. Fabien seeing her with a plate of salad sniffed scornfully.

"So, I'm living with a rabbit now," he said, bringing his face close to hers, making choppy chewing noises and showing his front teeth in imitation of a rabbit.

"And I a pig," retorted Glenda, "Oink oink!"

She stopped short and apologised, shamed by his shocked face.

Christmas and New Year were not happy times for Glenda. Her inner voice became more strident, and she had to admit that she'd happily moved in with someone whose way of life didn't suit her. She'd been flattered that gregarious, imperious Fabien had wanted to take her out to lovely restaurants. She had felt lucky to be his chosen one and he asked for nothing much of her in return. But, as with everyone, there was more to Glenda than 'nothing much' and now she was discovering the life she wanted to lead for herself. Fabien was pleased to have her at his side and unaware of all her self-analysis but then how could he be expected to notice. It wasn't his fault that she'd been masking dissatisfaction all these years.

A week into January, Glenda told Fabien that she wanted to go mountaineering every weekend and not miss any of the trips.

"There's just so much to discover," she tried to explain, hating her wheedling voice.

"Well, it's a mountain range, so there will be," Fabien shook his head, "but you're going to find that one peak looks like another, one lake exactly like another, one vista the same, same, same."

Getting Fabien to understand was as likely as Glenda being transfixed by sophisticated menus.

"They have names, they have stories…I love the way the sun on a slope brings out different facets from one minute to the next, the closeness of the sky. You should see it Fabien."

"I do see it," Fabien's disapproval was clear, "But I prefer to see it from a restaurant window. Why go to all that effort, when you can drink to it with a crisp, white Burgundy in good company from your comfortable seat?"

That was how different they were.

Glenda's heart was beating so hard, she thought he must be hearing it, seeing it pound.

"I have to do this," she gulped, "Fabien, I am doing this."

"Ok! You go ahead."

He gave a dismissive wave but his disbelieving smirk, which once would have withered her self-esteem, was losing its power over her.

Glenda became more proficient, stronger, and ever more passionate about her mountain trips. Often, on the way home, she stopped at a farm to buy fresh produce. One day, when the mother was collecting eggs for her, the children took her hand and lead her into the kitchen. It was warm and smelt of good, homely food. Seated at the table was a man they introduced as Remi, the shepherd. He smiled hello and to Glenda it seemed that his deep, brown eyes were like paths into a mysterious forest. His dog had eyes of sea-glass blue, eyes only for his master. Like Glenda's. He was very neat for a shepherd, Glenda thought. His chestnut hair and darker brown moustache looked recently trimmed and his hat and clothes were new and good quality. Comfortable-looking, durable clothes that looked good on him. He told her that he was helping on the farm during the winter and spring but soon it would be time to return to the mountain. He smiled fondly when he said this.

"Oh yes, I remember seeing all the sheep coming down from the mountains back in the autumn."

The shepherd nodded and told of his summers spent minding sheep and cows high up on the sweet-smelling herbage of the mountain slopes and how he was looking forward to returning to this natural life of air so pure and star-filled nights.

"A helicopter brings supplies for the season," he explained, stroking his dog who fell against him in delight, "So we don't miss out, do we Pasha?"

"The real highlife!" ventured Glenda and he smiled, acknowledging mutual understanding.

Like a mountain himself, she thought, *not attention-seeking, just there.*

"I make cheese," he went on, stroking his moustache and brought his knuckle close to his mouth, kissed it, demonstrating the taste of the cheese. "It sells in the top restaurants."

Glenda nodded and banished an unwanted vision of Fabien savouring top restaurant cheese. She sensed Remi floating up to grassy slopes against a backdrop of high peak skies.

"I love watching the eagles soaring. They make just the finest adjustments to their wing tips barely moving," he continued from far away, "but I must watch them," and he was back, wagging a shapely, bronzed finger at her. "Protecting the herd is our job. I mustn't lose any. There are other predators too. Bears have been reintroduced and wolves."

He watched Glenda's eyes widen and his own twinkled in amusement at the effect of his words on her. "Don't worry, everything is afraid of us. We walk upright and we might have a gun but a lamb or young calf, that's another matter."

"And you, do you have a gun?"

"Of course, but I've never needed to use it."

He smiled at her then corrected himself, "Except once!"

Glenda checked to see if he was joking and his smile broadened.

"I always feel safe. And it's another life up there. People ask if I get lonely or bored, but I don't. I learn something every day and there is always something different to see. It's not for everyone, but for me, it's the best life."

"It sounds lovely," breathed Glenda, "You're making me want to come too."

"So come."

She could tell he meant it.

"You should come for the walk up at least," he told her, "We always need extra shepherds to keep the troupe together. It's an early start but a great day, like a party. The animals are excited to be going up to the freedom of the mountain pastures. The town where we meet put on food and music for us and we set off. Then it's the music of the beasts and their bells and people echoing around the mountains and then it gets quieter and quieter as we come towards our summer home. Its moonlight when we arrive there."

As she drove home, Glenda was struck by how simply the equation of her life, unfathomably out of kilter all these years, suddenly seemed to fall into order.

Remi had told her that the passage of the sheep and cows to the high pastures would be at the beginning of June, so Glenda had two months to sort her life out.

Breaking up is never easy but is essential for lives to evolve. Fabien and Glenda broke up. Glenda moved out to a modest apartment. Shortly after, Martina moved in with Fabien and Geoff started looking around for a new girlfriend.

Glenda was surprised at the ease with which she arranged a three-month sabbatical from her office. Before dawn one

June morning, she parked her car in a hillside carpark and left it surrounded by empty livestock trucks. Disbelieving of her luck and senses alert to her surroundings, she set off with the shepherd, his dog, a troupe of sheep and herd of cows. The farmer's family and dogs, like Glenda were helping to keep the animals on the right tracks. Tracks so narrow at times that she worried the skittering animals might lose their footing and go tumbling down the sheer drop as did so many stones that their hooves dislodged. But no need to worry, these sure-footed beasts knew what they were doing. From behind, Glenda was bursting with a spirit of adventurous jubilation. She was reminded of the fable of the pied piper and understood the gleeful following. In the early hours of the next morning, they arrived at this humblest of homes. Everyone slept under the stars that night. Exhausted bodies melted into sleep. Glenda gazed up into the twinkling lights in the blue-black infinity, blotted out in places by the unseen bulk of rock. She had no idea how this was going to pan out but as her eyelids overruled her command to stay open, she knew, she was in exactly the right place at exactly the right time.

The Fish Dinner

How did we meet? On the beach of course. I was wading in the sun sprinkle shallows. How romantic is that? I'm lucky I know, living where I do. A fisherman's cottage built of ancient stone. The white-washed walls of my kitchen glow pink or orange as the sun goes down. Chilly and a little damp in winter, whiffs of mildew in my wardrobe, these are pence to pay. There's a rickety fenced garden where only carrots, fennel and sea thrift flourish. I cross the road and take the giant steps or the granite slab slipway down to powder soft sand. Sand turns shingle strewn with sea-rounded pebbles and scratchy dry seaweed and then there's the sea in all its blues and greens.

So we met and I surprised myself by inviting you to dinner and you accepted! We made arrangements. I would fetch you at six. Summertime, so long before the walls turn orange.

I spent a happy few hours preparing our dinner and at the appointed time came to find you. My heart was beating, *Will he be there?* I had doubts but of course you were.

What an evening!

Sea food, les fruits de mer. Sushi, mine with the pinpoints of wasabi you politely refused. Carefully rinsed seaweed tossed in garlicky oil or the plainer version, which was your preference as I had anticipated.

As we nibbled, we talked of our different lives. I was captivated by your stories and had to drag my gaze from your bold, dark eyes that spoke of ocean depths I would never know. My gaze dragged only as far as to your strong mouth, lingered there then returned with a force like magnetism to your eyes.

The bow tie wasn't necessary but added a debonair grace to your style. The black striped, blue-green of your fork tail ensemble was a handsome contrast to the silvery white beneath. Such an elegant figure in my humble kitchen. You found me beautiful too. I could sense your appreciation.

The walls turned orange and the brightness began to dim.

We found pleasure in the same music, although it remained a background to our conversation. You spoke of comraderies, communication through reflected light, the importance of orientation. Your tones turned sombre describing the constant need for vigilance; to be on the lookout for surprise and sustained attacks and I felt dread for you. To appease my disquiet, you diverted to sun warmed seas of easy living and I was reassured.

The time came as we knew it would. Sad but still glad to have known this brief sharing, we acknowledged that it was almost over.

I took you back to where I had found you. One kiss we shared, cold salty met hot garlic in this moment of sublime connection then we had to let go and you disappeared into the moon lit sea.

I swam for a long time, reminiscing, hopelessly willing you to reappear. Plankton blooms swirled, glowing and sparkling but I felt lonely even amidst the display which yesterday would have filled my souls with delight.

I grew cold. Time to return to the dry and the warmth. As I reached the shore a present touched my ankle. I scooped it up and smiled. Your bow tie. How thoughtful. It wreathes my wrist. I wear it always.

Lifecycles

It is during the Human Age, in Belfast, Ireland, on the 21st March 1922 that a baby boy is born, Arthur William Pattimore.

Ernest hates the wait. Daffodils dance in the park as he waits with first-born, Beryl, for the birthing to be done. Beryl totters around and he notices how she's changed, no longer a baby, Thank Goodness.

Beryl comes to rest before him "Mama," she mumbles then more plaintively, "Mama?"

He looks at his watch. "We can't go yet," he tells her and sighs at her tear-filled eyes, wishing there was someone else he could have left her with. He stands, "Come along then."

She walks beside him on chubby, determined legs. The sun shifts, its glare no longer broken by the branches, blinding Ernest as they amble along. When they get to the front door, Ernest is relieved to hear that the ordeal is over. Quicker this time. He looks in on Mary. Her eyes dance up at him, despite her labouring, and she captivates him all over again. He's relieved. Soon her body will return to normal and this time, she has born him a son.

By the time Arthur is two, he and Beryl have a baby brother, Clive, and the family have moved. Ernest is now a shopkeeper in the island of his birth. Mary can be heard singing and laughing from their home above the shop, which is on a hillside leading out of town. It's a good place. The lanes around town are crowded with families, all needing provisions, newspapers and tobacco. On Sundays, shops are shut. There is Mass and, if the weather is good, a walk around the park gardens or along the sea front.

Beryl holds Arthur's hand as she walks him up the road to his first day at school. Clive and little Molly are left at home with Mama's singing and tales. Arthur is quiet at first but soon settles. Stern paternal interest, Mama's cajoling and his own volition make him try hard at everything. He has a quick mind and is especially good at arithmetic. He is fast in running sports and his copperplate, quite beautiful.

It is a proud day for Ernest and Mary when Arthur takes his First Communion. So serious and scrubbed he looks, amongst the other pink-eared boys and white-laced girls. Both he, and later Clive become altar boys, Mary's angels. Mostly, it is a happy, industrious family. They sing and tease and share their good fortune with the poor by putting pennies in the velvet pouch at Collection.

Arthur's academic efforts are rewarded by a place at the Grammar School. The family have moved to a house with a garden further up the hill. Arthur is followed by Clive. Brotherly competition is encouraged by Ernest. Questions are to be answered if either son falls below third place when he comes to sign the ominously studied end of term reports.

Arthur leaves school at sixteen and begins working at a firm of accountants. He enrols at evening class for the required certification. While he is studying, his country goes to war and Molly is evacuated to England just days before the harbour is bombed and German soldiers come. The German occupiers import prisoners of war. These ragged, limping bags of bones are made to construct hideous fortifications along the coastlines, part of Hitler's Atlantic Wall. The beaches are made dangerous with land mines and barbed wire is unrolled along their edges. Shore foraging and fishing are forbidden. Fish stocks flourish.

Arthur had wanted to enlist with the other young men but was prevented by his place of birth. The recruiting officer was deaf to explanations and sent Arthur away with a flea in his ear. Desperate to do his bit for King and country, he sits on a wall near the harbour, nonchalantly drawing pictures of German machinery and taking note of their numbers. It's a dangerous pastime but the soldiers ignore this weedy, bespectacled youth.

Despite the curfew and list of civilian restrictions, Arthur falls in love with Ruth, only daughter of the town doctor. They meet because sister Beryl is ill. Medicine is restricted and the doctor is unable to treat Beryl. In peace times, she would have been taken by mail boat to a hospital on the mainland. It is terrible watching her become weaker and bedridden and pass away. Mary is distraught and only rallies when she receives a long-awaited letter from Molly, who is faring well with a kind lady in the countryside. Arthur and Ruth meet up whenever they can but, as with everything, their romance is on hold.

Towards the end of 1944, both locals and soldiers, are close to starvation. The German lines of supply have been severed by the Allies advance across Europe and the island is running out of everything. The Bailiff sends letters seeking aid from the Red Cross. The parsnip diet ends with cheers when the ship Vega makes the first of several trips bringing food parcels. The island is abuzz. The end of the war is in sight. The vanquished raise their heads. The occupiers taste defeat and those, who befriended the new losers, feel dread. Liberation Day is announced on 9 May 1945 but, for the Pattimore family, the war doesn't really end until July and Molly's return. They don't recognise each other at first, until Arthur cries out and makes a dive towards a strapping, taller Molly. She stares at her aged, scrawny family and has to fold Mother into her arms, when it should have been the other way around.

"But just look at you," Mary looks up at her, trying not to sob, "Our beautiful girl, home at last."

As soon as they can, Arthur and Ruth go on a much talked of motorbike trip. Their muscles are punished, and eyes opened to the destruction and delights of Europe. Infrastructure and lives are being rebuilt but the transition to peace is as long and painful as it is hopeful.

Upon their return, Arthur resumes his studies and Ruth works in a typing pool. One sunny day they have a picnic on a cliff top. They are stretched out on their wool rug when, suddenly but deliberately, Arthur pulls Ruth to a sitting position and kneels in front of her. He produces a ring that sparkles like the sea and asks Ruth to marry him. Her eyes sparkle like sea and ring, and she says "Yes, Arthur William Pattimore, I will marry you!"

They work and save until they can purchase a plot of land and, two years later, they are married and moving into their home.

Arthur and Ruth prosper. The house is extended to accommodate their children, Stephen, born in the summer of 1960 and Esther two years later. As Stephen and Esther grow, the island becomes a building site. The skyline of town changes. Ever bigger, more imposing buildings are ordered for the merchant banks. Great Britain joins the European Economic Area and the introduction of cheaper, if watery tomatoes and holiday destinations where drizzle and gales are not a feature, have put Guernsey out of fashion. The island is changing to a financial economy, the greenhouses falling into disrepair. Arthur is well placed to benefit from this change.

Stephen and Esther ride on the crest of the financial wave. They are aware that their lives are cushioned but with gains, there are always losses. Folk with time to chat after working their fields or potting in their boats, die out like the once thriving market. Farms and vineries, no longer viable, are sold and parcelled into plots for the burgeoning population. Big salaries and company perks change the feel. The island becomes smart, the roads congested, and no one seems to have time anymore.

Stephen then Esther finish school, learn to drive and head off to university in the UK. Stephen's hair and beard grow long, much to Grandfather Ernest's disgust. He has become cantankerous since Mary's demise and never forgives Molly for emigrating to New Zealand. He becomes Arthur and Ruth's problem. Clive and his wife got divorced so Ernest refuses to speak to Clive. Now he suspects that his grandchildren are heading down similar delinquent paths. His suspicions are confirmed when Stephen announces that he is heading for a year of surfing round the beaches of Europe. Shortly after Esther heads off to work on a Kibbutz in Israel.

Arthur bracing himself, takes Ernest to mass every Sunday. Afterwards, he and Ruth listen to Ernest's ranting and chewing. Ruth becomes anxious. She misses her breezy son, passionate daughter and cheery mother-in-law so much more than she will ever miss Ernest. Frail Ernest has a fall and it is decided that he must move in with them. These are the worst years of Ruth's life. Then, suddenly it's over. One morning, Ruth discovers that Ernest has passed peacefully away in his sleep. A blessing.

As if Ruth and Arthur are being rewarded for their goodness, first Stephen then Esther return home. Stephen gets his hair cut, marries lovely Kirstie and gets a job in a company that sells computers. Esther becomes a librarian. Arthur is now a partner of the accountancy firm, so he and

Ruth are able to help their children obtain mortgages. This is essential as the house prices continue to rocket.

Stephen and Kirstie have a daughter, Hattie and ten months later twin boys. Ruth and recently retired Arthur become doting grandparents. The family are knitted close, so much love and humour are shared with the boisterous, little people. Auntie Esther, another appreciated pair of hands, always arrives with stacks of carefully selected books.

Stephen parks up and makes his way through the security doors of the hospital. His training shoes squeak along the tiles of the glass covered walkway then become silent on the carpeted corridor leading to the palliative care ward. A moment of humour - his reflection shows his spectacles have stayed dark as he enters the ward. He feels as if he should have a white stick. Dark humour.

He sits in limbo beside Arthur, watching his laboured breathing. Prompted by the nurses, he tries to think of things to say to his dying father. It is the longest, loneliest hour.

After saying his final goodbye, Stephen sits in his car. He knew it was coming but feels shocked, a bereft orphan. With no one in between, Stephen has slipped, into the slow-slide-to-death slot. Through the windscreen clouds coil in and out of themselves in plump columns so white against the blue.

Stephen wonders about Hattie's daughter, Imogen, who was born into a body of the wrong gender. Imogen has a mentor at a special club and is to be referred to as *they*, not *she*. There is no more mass but Hattie religiously comes around for a coffee every Sunday morning. She patiently explains the intricacies of this baffling development to Stephen and Kirsty, such as she understands it. Watching the clouds, Stephen decides its a good thing that people get to live the lives they want to lead these days.

He wonders what Grandfather Ernest would have made of it. A Christmas scene fills his mind. A happier Ernest regaling stories of his army days, Grandma Mary, nestled next to him, a slightly perplexed smile brightening her still beautiful face. His thoughts turn back to Imogen and his heart lifts at this fresh, young being with her, no *their* darling, gap-tooth smile. He hopes he will see her, no *them*, now school has broken up. Its not so often these days.

Stephen takes the coast road home. He pulls into a sandy carpark and gets out, breathing in the briny fresh. Wonderful to banish those hospital smells. He allows himself to be soothed by the swishing waves. Memories tantalise, make him smile and weep. Childhood picnics and beach cricket. Arthur and Ruth, their juvenile selves still hovering, he and Esther ruthless to win and get ice-cream. Golden days in the passage of time.

Darkness and Bright

Ruby had always been anxious and timid with large, brown eyes continually glancing around for trouble. Early childhood had been blighted by living in London during the second world war. Ruby's civil engineer father George had been secreted away doing important work for the Ministry of Defence. Ruby's mother, deprived of her husband couldn't bear the thought of being separated from her home or daughter so they stayed together in the terraces of London. Still wearing terry nappies and big rubber pants Ruby's imagination was fired by the sombre voiced warnings emanating from the wheezy, crackling wireless. Ruby's mother tried to hide her fears with merry voice and bright smile but to Ruby her voice sounded shrill and she saw through the smile so the fears were shared. Cosy picture books contrasted with posters in the shops and underground tunnels warning of spies and admonishing waste.

George came home for occasional visits bringing excitement as well as chocolate and fruits, luxuries no longer available in the corner shop. On one such visit, George supervised the installation of an Anderson bomb shelter under a protective mound of earth in the back garden. After that there were frequent hurtles into the shelter to avoid the terrors of the blitz strikes. Ruby never stopped being afraid of darkness. Dark nights, dark corners, dark places. The dank smell of being submerged under dark earth was a recurring feature in her dreams. And spiders! Big ones that lurked and scuttled, made larger by their shadows in the torch or candlelight. She would always remember being just outside the shelter under blue sky, birds singing, roses blooming. Remember her mother's brown eyes searching the sky, the feel of being held in her mother's wool covered embrace as they heard the approach then watched the doodlebugs buzz overhead.

Protected…but if the buzz stops, you've had it. It happened on a street near theirs. The houses were left messily open to all, scorch blackened and the people who had lived in them were blown to bits.

Ruby was just seven when the war ended. Her father could come home at last but relief was short-lived because her mother became ill then died shortly before Ruby's eighth birthday. Before her ninth, Ruby had a stepmother. There was a bit of a ding dong because Ruby tearfully refused to call her anything other than what everyone else called her, Madge.

"You're to call her Mother," George insisted, "Show some respect!"

Ruby stood before him, fists bunched, tearfully refusing but Madge pulled George towards her, smiled into his eyes and quietly told him not to make a fuss. She bent to smile into Ruby's eyes, "How about a compromise?" and from then on Ruby happily called her Auntie Madge.

In the dreary grey of early peace Auntie Madge did her best with food rations, dashing off with her basket if the call came of fresh fish or apples or 'Bless us all', onions! Madge kept the house clean and homely and George in good spirits. She also kept the growing Ruby in expertly sewn, knitted and crocheted clothes so Ruby always felt nicely turned out. Auntie Madge was jolly, the door always open to neighbours for the sharing of tea, laughter and a sing song. Neighbourhood news was eagerly shared but meanness she nipped in the bud. The little family cuddled together and thrived. Ruby began to overcome her shyness. School, which she started late because of war time closures became less of an ordeal. She made friends, stuck her hand up to answer questions and came home with end of term reports praising her contributions in class. Meanwhile rubble was being swept into piles as the rebuild teams got to work. What could be salvaged was sorted from the beyond ruined. To help overcome the labour shortage, the government invited folk from the Commonwealth to come to rebuild Britain. The first time Ruby came across these new, dark faces, she was so scared that she wet herself. Terrors experienced before she had words to express them became associated with the immigrants and if she couldn't avoid them altogether, she would slink or run past even though they paid her no heed.

At fifteen Ruby got a job as assistant in a chemist's shop. The chemist knew the family and was patient with Ruby's initial timidity. As she got to know the customers Ruby gained in confidence. She was as careful and conscientious as her teacher's reference had promised and understood the requirement for discretion. The ravages of war were becoming less evident and it was an optimistic time in London. Ruby often went to the theatre or new picture houses with her young friends or Madge. At last suspicion, watchfulness and retribution could be put aside. Gaiety prevailed. On fine days Ruby and Madge might go and listen to the speakers in Hyde Park and titter at some of the more outlandish ranting.

When Ruby was seventeen, George died suddenly of a heart attack. She and Madge helped each other through the shock and Ruby watched Madge change from being wife to widow. One of the highlights of Ruby's life was going to the dance halls. After a respectful time of mourning, Madge agreed to take Ruby and they began going every Saturday. Under Madge's watchful eye, Ruby and her friends were invited to dance and chat with the young men at the hall. Madge was watching when a certain Harry Benson exchanged a glance with Ruby and they both smiled. The smiling didn't stop. Ruby couldn't believe that out of all the pretty girls fluttering around, Harry liked her. Harry was handsome but didn't seem to know it. Everyone liked him because he was always cracking jokes and had a way of teasing so that a person felt special, not belittled. Harry was an insurance salesman. A respected one. What Ruby loved about him was his ability to make her feel that everything was going to be alright. Harry made Ruby feel safe and cherished and he made her laugh a lot. Ruby shone. Madge and Ruby had many 'Harry' conversations during the ensuing courtship.

Shortly before Ruby's twentieth birthday, Harry asked Madge if she would give her permission for him to propose to Ruby. Responsibility for this decision weighed heavily on Madge. She asked Harry many questions before giving her consent. Harry was compelled to reveal his serious side and prove his worth. After this rigorous grilling, Madge went for a think about it in the back garden. An anxious Harry watched her pacing around the neat lawn as if in conversation with herself but when she came back in, she was smiling. A week later a thrilled Ruby was showing off her engagement ring. It was a modest but happy wedding day. Madge was Maid-of-Honour and walked Ruby down the aisle. It made sense that Harry would move in with Ruby and Madge. The next summer a new member of the family was sleeping in a lace-fringed pram with three besotted adults oohing and aahing over her. Baby Claire.

After her childhood setbacks, it seemed to Ruby that she was now having all the luck. Little Claire had the usual childhood health scares but was healthy in the main and as loving as she was loved. At school, she was diligent and popular and made her parents proud. As Ruby had the highly trusted Madge to look after Claire, she decided to get a part-time job. Her position as hotel receptionist, earned not just a wage but a sense of self-worth, she never would have expected to feel. Harry was doing well too, heading up a small insurance office and they were able to extend the house to make a bit more space for themselves and have summer holidays on the coast. The family of four always ate together and kept each other abreast of developments in the world around them, which was changing at an ever-faster pace. Lively discussions around the tea table revolved around the politics of the day, the beloved Royal family, shenanigans of the famous and the mind-boggling marches of progress. There were changes locally too. Families no longer seemed rooted in the terraces and as people moved out, often it was black families who moved in. Ruby ignored them, they were irrelevant and she and her precious family were happy in their bubble. Until just after Harry's forty-ninth birthday.

Odd, how you don't notice little changes until they add up to something that needs attending to. They were all missing Claire, who had decided to study for her chemistry degree in York of all the far-flung places. Harry began feeling tired and irritable, couldn't find the word he was thinking of. He became forgetful and would get confused and frustrated about silly things. So unlike Harry. Ruby became anxious again, her eyes glaring around for trouble. It was Madge, now wearing round-rimmed spectacles and thick wool tights all year, who suggested making a doctor's appointment. After further appointments and tests the doctor diagnosed that Harry was suffering from pre-senile dementia and Ruby felt her world which had been shaking more and more wildly, flip over and squash her underneath.

Harry's famous glee-shared sparkle became replaced with a fiendish, furtive gleam. His behaviour became stranger and increasingly difficult to cope with. They both had to hand in their resignations and knew the isolation was terminal. Ruby shed many tears coming to terms with the fact that he wasn't going to get better. She was losing him. Day by day a little more of Harry was replaced with this spectre who had nothing to do with the man she loved. She was on edge all the time because he kept slipping out the door. One minute dozing in his chair, the next gone. He could be lost for hours, Ruby calling and calling as she made larger and more desperate circles around the house. In addition to the panic of losing Harry, Ruby was frightened of the streets surrounding her home. Gone were the people she knew. The new neighbours all had dark faces that brought back childish terrors. The newspapers flamed her mistrust, bellowing accusations of violence, drugs and burglaries.

Ruby scuttled the streets offended by unfamiliar music, voices and cooking aromas. She hardly dared to look into the gardens, let alone ask for help. She kept dashing up to her front door, relieved to escape the street and praying he'd found his way home. Often it was the police who brought him back in better or worse states of indignity. They were patient enough but she felt admonished by her failure of care. One day a combination of exhaustion and frustration made Ruby lose her temper and shout at Harry. He had somehow found the key she'd hidden and she ran to stop him opening the back door. Harry thumped Ruby, sending her flying. Trust was gone for good and not long after that, time came for Harry to be moved to a nursing home. Guilt competed with relief. The home involved bus and tube rides but Ruby went every single day. It was a depressing place and Harry was deteriorating fast. Ruby felt suspicious of some of the staff. Bruises and grazes were explained by falls. His balance was worsening but surely that was what they were paid to prevent? It vexed her that some of the staff danced to tunes on the radio while feeding those residents who could no longer feed themselves. It was an absent-minded, swaying dance in between mouthfuls that looked comfortable and Ruby found utterly inappropriate. She complained to the Ward Sister. Sister Mary heard her out patiently but explained that all the staff, irrespective of skin-colour were appropriately qualified. Having music in the dining room cheered everybody up. Harry's care would be carried out by the staff on duty at the time. She could promise that his professional carers would treat him with kindness and respect. Ruby, thwarted and defeated, was engulfed by a horrible sobbing episode. Mary waited until the worst was over then stuck her head out of the office door and called Dobbs to please bring Ruby a cup of tea. Dobbs, it turned out was a lean, black woman whom Ruby had seen working on the ward. She had a rather dour mien. Dobbs didn't dance. Ruby was taken aback that Mary had called the nurse by her surname but assumed this was the norm. The teacup, she noticed was so clean it squeaked and the tea good and hot and comforting.

Claire's weekly phone calls and Madge's enduring love kept Ruby sane. Claire was now doing a post-graduate degree. She was working to fund her studies so home visits were rare. Claire adored her family, knew how much her absence was missed but loved her life in York. On visits she stoically accompanied Ruby to the home but overtime Harry's precious glimmer of recognition faded to a dull stare. All the dull stares in the room seemed to fix on pretty, youthful Claire. As if the demise of her father wasn't bad enough, Claire was also finding time spent with her mother difficult.

"They're just people Mum," she would say after one of Ruby's tirades on the way the blacks had taken over her neighbourhood.

"Its alright for you, you live in York," Ruby snapped.

"Mum, I study and work with people of all race and creed, they're lovely and intelligent and hardworking," Claire insisted.

"Not round here, they're not!" Ruby snatched up the newspaper and shoved it at Claire, "See! Rioting and looting. There's always been trouble ever since they got here."

Claire glanced at the photos of police in riot gear, not only, but mainly black youths hurling anything they could grab at them against the backdrop of burnt-out cars.

"Mum!" Claire sighed, "That's Brixton, not round here." She stuck the paper in the magazine rack, glancing at it again as she did so. "I mean, its dreadful but they're angry because they live in bad housing, no jobs, no hope and the police, some of the police, are downright racist. That new 'Stop and Search' bill, they're too heavy handed. There's another side to this. I've told you before if you only read this paper… it's biased, it doesn't explain both sides of the story. Why not read a different paper every day? Get a change of perspective."

Ruby didn't want to hear and certainly didn't want to evoke unnecessary dialogue with the new owner of the corner shop. She always felt dirty when she was in there since he took over with his weird spices and ridiculous bananas.

"What difference would that make? If it was up to me they'd all be sent straight back to where they came from."

"Mum, these are young, they were born here, they deserve to have the same rights as you and me."

Madge's voice was querulous these days but she was still one for keeping the peace. "I think its what the person is like on the inside that matters…"

Ruby sprang up with a snarl of frustration, slammed out the door and stomped around the unmown back garden. She was enraged further that her stomping was beating time with the ska music jangling out from her neighbours' boombox. How could they gang up on her like that? She just betted they were talking about her. But she knew better than them. Stomp, stomp. She knew!

Claire's visits became even more infrequent after that but two visits that couldn't be avoided involved funerals. Harry caught a winter chill and succumbed to pneumonia. Ruby gazed at him for hours as he laboured his last. She tried resurrecting memories from happier times but as his death rattle announced the end she felt as much of a husk as he was.

Madge valiantly rose to the occasion, insisting on new clothes, hairdressers and colourful flowers.

"A drop of sherry," Madge said, handing out a glass to Ruby and Claire as they waited for the funeral car, "We need a bit of fortification for today, don't we. Drink up Ruby."

She stood between mother and daughter at the funeral like a stalwart fairy and sang like a bird. After Claire's departure, Madge who hadn't been out for months now insisted on accompanying Ruby to the shops chirpily singing out good mornings to all and sundry as they went, beaming at the bus drivers who waited for her and conductors who helped her up the bus steps. She was always offered a seat. Not so Ruby.

It was March, Madge pointed out the daffodils and tulips as they passed the park on the way home. They'd had Best Bristol Bangers and Mash and a sherry in the Black Lantern and then done the weekly shop. Ruby opened the door, hung up her coat and started putting things away.

Madge plumped herself down on the chair that slotted in next to the fridge.

"I'm feeling a bit tired," she said, "I'll just sit down a minute, then I'll take my coat off and put the kettle on."

A little while later when Ruby went her to wake her, she realised that Madge had died, just like that. Shock hardened Ruby couldn't even cry, in fact couldn't seem to do anything. Claire came home and it was up to her to make the funeral arrangements, Ruby nodding grimly at any input she was asked to make. It was a quiet affair, the friends all gone as well as the songbird.

Ruby stared at life, as might a stick insect on a twig of privet in a tank.

"You have to get out Mum," Claire breathed down the telephone, "Join the library, tell me about the books you're reading or get a job. You're still young you know."

Ruby almost vomited the bitter ball of angst at her core in response to Claire's optimism. Why couldn't she make Claire listen. Ruby only left the house for essentials these days. There was only one other white in the terrace now. Mad Olive who lived with an enormous and fierce Alsatian dog. Olive wasn't her real name but they'd always called her that after Harry pointed out how much she looked like Popeye's wife. These days she always looked like cross Olive. When the dog had been a more manageable size, she'd told Ruby, she'd got him for protection. The dog stayed in the house these days, barking and hurling itself against the door when people passed the gate. Olive could be heard screaming at him to let her in or out of the house.

"Laddie! Its me you idiot. Laddie! Let me in!" Shopping would go flying as she cursed and forced and barged her way past door and dog.

If Ruby crossed paths with anyone during one of Olive's entries, she kept her eyes downcast. How dare they snigger at a fellow white? But then Ruby always kept her eyes downcast. These days it was Ruby who was irrelevant.

One March morning Ruby decided to go to see the flowers in the park. They might remind her of happier times. On the way she was astonished to bump into someone she knew.

"Lorna!"

"Ruby! How lovely to see you. This is my friend, Clive. We're just heading to church. Is that where you're going? Its always such a lovely service here isn't it."

Ruby was so delighted to see a familiar face that she tagged along. It felt good to be going to church with these two decent people but when she walked in Ruby wanted to walk straight back out again. The congregation was black, even the vicar was black. Sandwiched between Lorna and Clive, Ruby's eyes were everywhere as the organ started up.

"I just love the singing don't you," Lorna smiled at Ruby.

Ruby could only stair ahead, she couldn't wait to get out of there but as the jubilant singing got going, she closed her eyes and her ears couldn't help but listen. There was goodness in this room. All the goodness of Harry. Tears squeezed out and down her cheeks. 'Harry, I miss you, I miss you so much.'

Lorna noticed and put a comforting arm around Ruby. Clive handed over his handkerchief, big and manly. By the end of the service tears still threatened but Ruby had pulled herself together sufficiently to shake hands with the gently smiling vicar. She was reluctant but manners mattered. Clive and Lorna took her for coffee and a big slab of cake then walked through the flower bordered park with her, absorbing her loneliness and sharing their own losses.

They became a gang of three after that. Ruby lunched with them every day and they went to the theatre, exhibitions and occasionally on out-of-town excursions. Ruby was pleased to tell Claire that they even went to the library together. Claire was delighted. Such a relief that a corner had at last been turned. At church one Sunday Lorna and Clive became very excited because there had been an announcement that the annual party would be going ahead as usual.

"Carnival! You must come. Its brilliant!" Lorna enthused. "You'll love it. There's music and dancing and lovely food. They even get special permission for a bar and I thoroughly recommend the rum punch."

Ruby couldn't hide her alarm "What like Notting Hill?"

Clive was reassuring and as always more circumspect. "No, no, hardly! Its in the church hall but they go to so much trouble decorating it and what have you. It really is quite a spectacle but there's always a lovely friendly atmosphere and it finishes at eleven so doesn't get out of hand. Not like Notting Hill at all really."

Ruby said she'd think about it, already knowing she had no intention of going but Lorna worked on her and one March evening she found herself accompanying them. It was mad! So warm compared to the chill outside. Lorna had been right about wearing a blouse and cardigan so as not to overheat. Palm tree-painted cloths and seascapes hung on the walls, steel band music jangled, exotic food smells wafted. There was even a sandy beach tucked in a corner. Such clothes! Such hair! Dazzling patterns, even the men! Feathers, costumes, glittering make-up. Ruby had never seen the like. Shiny-eyed laughter, and exuberant joshing. Ruby gazed around, feeling as if she'd gate-crashed a film set. Clive handed her a glass of the famous punch.

"Take it easy," he cautioned its stronger than you think."

"Cheers!" sang Lorna "Here's to some fun!"

The drink was sweet, tasting of pineapples and coconut and the rum that was pleasantly relaxing. Ruby's mad glancing calmed down. There were a few other white faces she noticed but they were very much the minority. Was she safe? It all seemed friendly enough now but later? Clive stayed next to Ruby but Lorna was off chatting and laughing, easily fitting in with everyone. People came up to chat with Clive. He introduced Ruby to Ken, his wife Charmagne and their young daughters, Dania and Ines. Then it was Elaine and Royston, and their teenage sons Steven and Rodney who smiled shyly even though wearing the enormous caps that had always suggested trouble to Ruby. There were others, too many names to take in. Ruby smiled, saying little but the smiles came more easily and broadened as she got used to the different hair and skin tones and scents. Dark, different but friendly and decent and polite. These were respectable people who cared for their families as much…as much as herself!

Ruby refused a second glass of punch, preferring to stay on the safe side. As they approached the buffet table she stared at the big dishes of rice and God knows what in trepidation.

Lorna filled her plate for her, "Ooh and you must try this!" she kept saying adding another spoonful to the heaps. They took their plates and found a table near the 'beach.' Ruby was surprised at how much she enjoyed it for all the spiciness and unidentifiable flavours.

"Gorgeous isn't it. Mmm." Lorna was talking with her mouth full, clearly the punch was going down as well as the food.

"Good to see you're enjoying yourself tonight Ruby," Clive said.

Ruby nodded. She looked around at the happy, lively people, eating and drinking. Surprisingly, she was.

"Goodness, I can feel myself putting on weight." Ruby told the others.

"Don't worry about that," Lorna laughed. "We'll be dancing it off soon."

Ruby thought not. "You go, I'll watch," she told them when the band got going and the floor was cleared for dancing.

The music wasn't quite her thing. She watched Clive and Lorna enthusiastically jigging amongst the more supple, graceful dancing. Harry would have loved this. Ken and Charmagne were dancing, their girls with them. Elaine and Royston too. Steven and Rodney were not on the dancefloor but horsing around with some other boys, swapping caps and throwing them in the air. As one song ended, Charmagne said something to Ken and he came over to Ruby, asking her to dance.

"Charmagne needs a rest," he told Ruby, "She thought you might like to dance."

"Oh! Well..." To decline would have been publicly rude so Ruby stood and Ken led her by chivalrous hand to the floor. It was a slower number so Ken drew her to him, put his hand on the small of her back and they waltzed through the song. Ruby felt herself in some sort of sensorial kaleidoscope. To be so close, to feel and smell, washing powder and warm black skin, really see up close, clean and it was...so nice! Ken was a man she could trust. Ruby felt herself relax. As they turned, she caught Charmagne's eye and they smiled at each other. The little girls were beside their mother covering their mouths, giggling. At the end of the song, Ruby thanked Ken and he smiled, took her back to her table, made a slight bow and went back to his family.

Lorna and Clive were still jigging. Faces were glowing and perspiring. Ruby furtively looked at her watch. She suddenly felt terribly alone as if the thrill of dancing had shed light on something she'd been keeping shrouded in the dark. Her eyes filled, "Damn! Don't you dare put the damper on things." She took a tissue from her bag and dabbed surreptitiously. Then Ruby looked up surprised that someone was standing in front of her. The woman she recognised as Dobbs from the Home.

Dobbs was looking at her sternly then patted Ruby's hand with her own. "Come on," she said, "Lets go somewhere we can talk."

Ruby was so astonished that she rose and obeyed. Dobbs led her to seats near the now deserted beach.

"You're missing your husband," Dobbs looked at Ruby in a way that could be concerned or could be disapproving, "He was a good man. I can always tell." She gave Ruby a knowing nod. "I'm sorry for your loss."

Ruby thanked Dobbs for the care she had shown Harry.

Dobbs nodded. She had a quiet wisdom about her.

"I'm sorry, but what's your name again?" Ruby asked.

Dobbs looked at her, "You can call me Dobbs," she said levelly then turned and nodded at a boy in a way that bade him come over. He looked a bit sullen.

"Jerome, would you please go and fetch us a glass of ice cubes from the bar?"

He turned and disappeared into the crowd but was quickly back again setting the glass of ice on their table.

"Thank you, Jerome," said Dobbs warmly and he smiled shyly.

"Thank you," Ruby added and the smile broadened lighting up his face. Strange but it was almost as if he were relieved to hear her say that, as if the lack of trust, the fear was mutual.

"No problem," he said quietly, then went to rejoin his friends.

Trust, thought Ruby, *has to start somewhere. If it wasn't for Dobbs I would never have known.*

Dobbs removed a bottle of rum from her bag and two smaller glasses. She put a lump of ice in each and covered it with rum. She handed a glass to Ruby.

"Sip it," she said firmly and took a little sip of hers.

Ruby did the same.

"It's good," Dobbs told her.

She sat back studying Ruby.

"I'm a widow too."

She looked up as if annoyed by a small detail, "Kind of."

She held Ruby in her gaze.

"I know how it feels."

Her eyes misted momentarily, "Too young,"

Her eyes dipped and levelled up again. "Far too young."

Ruby stared back, "What was his name?"

It was all she could think of to say.

Dobbs looked sterner than ever then her face softened.

"Laurence Arthur Marshall."

She pronounced every syllable with care then turned to her handbag and took from it a photograph which she held to show Ruby. A handsome young man with intelligent eyes smiled up at her.

Dobbs carefully placed the photograph back in her bag.

"He was head boy at the school."

Ruby could hear the pride.

Dobbs was smiling but the corners of her mouth were turned down.

"He was my fiancé. We were to be married."

She picked up her glass and took a little sip. Ruby did the same.

"He was working on the night bus,"

Dobbs had very graceful fingers.

Her eyes went very dark, "There are people who don't like us because of the colour of our skin."

Ruby's heart was beating ominously.

"Some of those people took offence at Laurence."

Her gaze was relentless.

Ruby didn't want to hear this.

"When he was on his way home from his shift, they…" Dobbs shook her head. "They attacked him. They beat him to death."

She smiled at Ruby. All the pain of loss, bewilderment and longing were held in that sad smile.

Ruby wanted to negate what she had heard. There were no words of comfort she could offer. Shame, pettiness, stupidity. Her face registered outrage.

Dobbs made a sign and they both took a sip. It was the last sip.

Dobbs squared her shoulders. "It helps sometimes to share a little rum with someone who understands."

She emptied the remaining ice from her glasses into the other glass.

"Maybe we'll do it again sometime."

"I'd like that. Thank you, Dobbs,"

Dobbs nodded, stood up and taking her bag and the glasses walked away. Ruby watched her thread through the crowd as always poised and erect. All Dobbs had was her dignity and her job looking after white people in the latter stages of dementia. Ruby sat quietly ruminating on what she had heard until Lorna bounded over shouting, "Here you are!"

When Ruby got home, it was if she was seeing it after waking from a long and drudging dream. All the memories, all the love and laughter. Her mother and George and wonderful Madge. Claire from baby to woman and all that time with the man she loved. Up in her room, she sat at her dressing table gazing at the photograph of her and Harry. They were sweethearts like Laurence and Dobbs had been.

She picked it up, "Oh Harry," she told him, "Haven't we been lucky!"

The Love of Mothers

Henry Stopes was an unusual eight-year-old, who communicated by whoops, growls and trills that only his devoted mother, Sheila could understand. During the tempestuous years of Henry's childhood, which had seen off his father after only two, Sheila noticed that Henry was at his happiest on the seashore. These days, he especially loved the cliff bays, which were usually deserted because of their difficult access. Sheila would follow, urging caution down dangerously steep paths, marvelling at Henry's easy scramble. Once there, she could relax watching the love of her life potter about on the soft sand or in seaweed fronded pools. In the protective embrace of the cliff, Henry's spirit could roam free. He wasn't a strong swimmer, but the sea was gentle and clear, turning turquoise to blue to meet the sky. With her boy so easily amused, Sheila's thoughts could turn to other things but not for long, Henry's safety was paramount. Sometimes, during these brief reveries, she revisited her office years. Inevitably, her thoughts would turn to her old boss, Deirdre Barrett. Sheila had liked Deirdre, recognising a kindred, sensitive soul, and Sheila would wonder what on earth could have happened to her.

Deirdre Barrett was never going to be pretty. An only child, her mother first informed her of this when she was just four years old. Mrs Barrett had firmly counselled that she'd better work hard at school. Marriage seemed unlikely so she was going to have to be independent. This truth had been crystalised by very pretty Emily Blythe when the girls were nine. Observant and heartless, Emily had declared Deirdre's eyes too close-set, her mouth too small and her nose, just weird. In addition to these aesthetic deficiencies, was the effect Deirdre had on other people. This had started with her parents, especially her father, whose profound irritation at her mere presence in the room, meant that Deirdre was never going to make it as a social success. She did work hard at school, mainly because the only girl who tolerated her as a desk share, was the class swot. Deirdre came second best at everything. Everything except sport. At netball, hockey and swimming she was ranked below even the class swot.

The qualifications gained led to a good job in a small office. Deirdre stayed put. The office grew and her loyalty led to promotion and ultimately meant she could afford to buy her own house, a nice one, out of town, near the cliffs. She shared her home with Tibby, a now fat and elderly cat, her only source of affection. The barely concealed amusement of her colleagues towards her had softened over the years. They no longer called her (not quite behind her back) 'Dreary', and she felt accepted by her fellow long-stayers as the reliable oddity that was Deirdre.

On wet days, Deirdre took her monotonously packed Tupperwares to the library and read through her lunchbreak. If it was dry, she went to the public gardens and, in the shade of the rhododendrons, watched the birds while she munched or gazed about at the flowers or few people that came by. Her former tight-lipped envy at couples holding hands or canoodling under the trees had turned these days into a wistful interest.

During Deirdre's late thirties, a new regular began coming to the gardens. A tall man. A fellow loner, who leant over the wrought-iron railings surrounding the fishpond gazing into its depths or sat brooding on the shadier bench next to hers. After several days of rain, he nodded at Deirdre and expressed relief at the more clement weather. After that, they always passed the time of day. Deirdre found she looked forward to lunchtimes more, and gradually, the greetings turned to little chats and soon they were sitting on the same bench. The man never ate, politely refusing Deirdre's offer of a sandwich, so she continued to eat alone. Deirdre was surprised to discover that such a handsome man was like her, unmarried and felt intimidated in social settings. His name, like the name of her handbag, was Bryan. He had a foreign air about him, slightly sallow of skin with shadows under his eyes and dark thinning hair. He stooped a bit when he walked, which Deirdre found endearing. One day, Bryan surprised Deirdre by taking her hand and kissing it. After that he would put quick kisses on her lips when they first saw or left each other. Deirdre found herself daring to think that perhaps her mother had been wrong after all.

It was a good thing that Bryan had come into Deirdre's life because Tibby was coming to the end of his. During the last of a series of early morning appointments, Deirdre was guided by the vet to make the terrible decision, and Tibby was put to sleep. After a tearful morning at her desk, Deirdre felt relieved to be going outside at noon. It was a clear day and Bryan was waiting for her. He was kind and didn't seem to mind Deirdre sobbing into his chest. Deirdre was comforted and distracted. Bryan's scent was unusual. Bizarrely, she was reminded of a school trip to a historic tower. Deirdre was struck by a memory of Emily Blythe, hysterical after a bat had had to be cut out of her blonde curls. Deirdre sat up. Bryan gave her his handkerchief and she wiped her face and smiled gratefully up at him.

Towards the end of one lunchtime, Bryan asked Deirdre if she could come back after work. It was still warm as she walked up the path to meet him, but the roses had had their day and the lupins had turned to pods. As she approached, Deirdre noticed that Bryan was looking even more pensive than usual. When she sat down, he told her that he was going to have to go away for a while because he was unwell. He promised he would return as soon as he could, Deirdre scrutinizing his face, which was indeed pale. Bryan gently kissed the tears tracing down Deirdre's cheeks then stood and led her by the hand through a path in the bamboos. He laid her down on a bed of the dried leaves and without protest, Deirdre allowed him to do whatever he wanted while the bamboos rustled all around. They stayed in the gardens until the moon was shining on the pond. When the night turned chill, Bryan walked Deirdre to the gates, and they went their separate ways. Deirdre, in a state of elated and devastated shock, found herself praying for his recovery and clinging to his promise to return.

Several weeks later, Deirdre perceived changes in her body. A hunger for foods she never ate and an abhorrence of others. Her breasts became heavy, her stomach cramped. After a furtive trip to a chemist, Deirdre sat staring at the result of her pregnancy test. It was hardly conclusive.

During a sleepless night, she reread the instructions several times. Blue not green. Her line had been green as a wine bottle. In the morning, she gazed at the instructions and reader a moment longer then threw it all in the bin and drove herself to work. Deirdre knew she should contact her doctor, but something prevented her from doing so and she carried on as if nothing was happening.

One evening, Deirdre began feeling unwell. She took off her nightie and stared at her abdomen in the bedroom mirror. Her breasts were enormous, their raised nipples almost black. Her abdomen began rippling and she swayed back and forth stroking it. Pains, from what she'd read, labour pains, began wracking her body. She swayed and sweated, panted and groaned. She moved into her bathroom, splashing cold water over herself. Urges to squat and push became more regular, more forceful and frantic until she felt a body pass through and out on to the bathroom floor. She stared down at what she had borne. Surely too early for a healthy baby and such a strange shape, like a small torpedo of purple, veiny flesh. She picked it up, warm and pulsating, cuddling it to her. She detected movement and sat on the toilet seat lid, holding it in her lap. As she crooned and massaged it, it began changing shape. Into shapes! Into the shapes of creatures. Bats! First one then a second emerged and so on until Deirdre realised that she had given birth to six beautiful bats. She gazed at them, their little bodies and perfect folded wings. They peeped up at her, their tiny squeaks engorging her breasts and setting milk spurting from her nipples. Carefully, Deirdre eased herself down on the bathmat and helped her babies find the milk dribbles. They clung to her with soft claws, seeking, finding, drinking and Deirdre was overcome with devotion.

The babies grew. Deirdre emptied her larder and freezer to keep them in milk. They were doing so well. Her six joys. She knew, she would do anything, lay down her life for them and she began to worry. What if they were discovered? Her fretting was heightened one evening when the doorbell rang. She flung her dressing-gown over her latched-on babies and opened the door, just a crack.

It was Vincent from the office.

"Hello Deirdre," he said, peering to make eye-contact, "Sorry to bother you but we were getting worried. Are you alright?"

"Yes, well, getting better now. Sorry, I should have called in. Awful virus. I'll send in the doctor's certificate tomorrow. Sorry."

At the mention of the certificate, Vincent relaxed.

"Oh no. That's alright. When you're ready. Don't worry, just bring it in when you come back. You look after yourself and get yourself better Deirdre."

He gave a smiley nod then turned and trotted to his car. Deirdre locked the door. She shrugged off the dressing gown and stared at herself in the hall mirror. She shone pale in the gloomy light, her six loved ones hanging from her breasts, sucking hard. Something had to be done. The house was not fortress enough.

Deirdre put on her trainers and covered her brood with a mac. Cuddling them to her skin, she went out through the back garden to the cliff path. As if being summonsed, she followed the paths down. Progress was slow. Gulls and crows menaced around calling out threats. At last, she reached the slippery stones of the shoreline. Her eyes sought out and found the cave entrance and she went in and followed the cave back until it became dry. At times, Deirdre had to put the protesting babies before her so she could squeeze between or under rocky outcrops, grazing her skin along the way. The mac, no longer useful, was discarded. Once through, she'd scoop them up and warm them to her again. When she could go no further, she wedged herself between two rocks, leant against the back wall and let them feed. Silently, from the shadows, their father came to greet them.

It was a warm day and being a spring tide, young Henry Stopes found new places to explore. He saw a cave just as Mother called him for lunch. Henry went in anyway, but it became too dark to see, so he turned and ran to her, remembering the telephone she sometimes allowed him when he was upset. As well as the games, the telephone had a torch. When Sheila was packing away the lunch things, Henry snatched up the phone and sprinted down the beach. Sheila watched him run, how she loved this strange boy. The rock at her back was warm and Sheila allowed her tired eyes to close, just for a moment.

Now that he could see, Henry's small, sinuous body made quick progress through the cave. Amongst the drier rocks and shale, his feet suddenly met with something soft. Material here? Strange! What was that white ahead of him? Wide-eyed, Henry stared at the grinning skeleton before him. It was wearing training shoes. He'd thought the ribcage had holes in it but now could see that there were three large bats hanging from one side, four from the other. Henry gawped. These bones weren't smooth, but covered in tiny, serrated ridges. The bats became twitchy. They didn't like this light, but they did like this smell. They stretched their wings and took flight, dipping in and out of the torchlight. They began dive-bombing Henry. As he turned to flee, Henry raised his arms to protect himself from the leathered wings slapping his head and sharp fangs making incisions in his scalp. The phone went clattering away.

Sheila awoke and, berating herself, ran to follow Henry's footprints in the sand. Desperately searching and full of dread Sheila saw that the tide had turned. At the water's edge, the footprints disappeared, only stones. Suddenly, Sheila's glancing, seeking eyes, fell upon Henry's bloodied figure emerging from the cave, sploshing into the rising sea. Black shapes were flying at him, attacking her boy. Enraged at this assault on his body, Sheila ran roaring towards him, slipping on the algae covered stones. The cuts to her feet and knees didn't even register, she was so astonished, horrified and filled with maternal instinct at hearing Henry utter his first proper words…

"Mamma! Help me!"

Ace of Cups - A Christmas Tale

Margaret McGrath opened the door to Number 52 and breathed a sigh of relief. The door brushed the mat as she pushed it closed, such a familiar sound, like the welcome of a loved one. Margaret felt her way along the chilly hall to the kitchen door frame. She stopped and her hand felt the inside wall for the light switch. As the hum and buzz fluorescent flashes lit up the even chillier kitchen, a soft warmth caressed Margaret's puffed-up calves.

"Hello Tinks!" Margaret put down her holdall and stiffly stooped to stroke the fluff covered bones of her elderly housemate.

"Treats Mr Tinks!" Margaret set the holdall on the weary formica, unzipped it and took from its mustard sturdiness a box of mince pies, a carton of custard and a box shouting cheerfully of the chocolates within. She felt around and retrieved a tin of pilchards.

"Oh My, Mr Tinks! This is going to be the best Christmas for a long time."

Margaret had moved into Number 52 as Bob's young bride during the times known as the Swinging Sixties, a notion which had remained as foreign to her and Bob as the notion of honeymooning in Italy or flying to the moon. Their marriage had taken place at Hounslow registry office. Bob's widowed mother and Margaret's widower father were their witnesses and she had moved in with Bob and Mrs McGrath, (in Margaret's young eyes, the real one) that afternoon. Her father's wedding present had been this very holdall. He'd said it was a good one.

Bob and Margaret were well suited to each other. Bob had worked as a bin man and Margaret was a cleaner. She had started her first cleaning job in the department store when she was just fifteen and stayed working there all her life. Neither Bob nor Margaret had much of a head for figures but they were hardworking and decent and loyal. On account of their different work schedules, the newlyweds didn't see that much of each other, but when they did, it was nice and they especially liked going to the flicks and for a special treat, the funfair. Margaret was glad Mrs McGrath seemed to like her too and did her best to fit in and be helpful. Sadly, Bob had been taken from them in a shockingly sudden way. Margaret had come home from work one day to find policemen in the sitting room and Mrs McGrath in tears. Margaret's grey all-noticing, nothing-telling eyes blinked hard as one policeman explained that

Bob had been killed during his rounds that morning. He had been the victim of a hit and run incident and had died at the scene.

Bob hadn't suffered, the other policeman wanted her to know.

The first policeman promised both Mrs McGraths that they would follow all possible leads to find the driver, but they never saw or heard from them again. Neither of the two ladies in Bob's life ever fully recovered.

Margaret put the tin of pilchards away in the cat food section of the cupboard.

"We must wait for tomorrow," she told Tinks, who responded with a plaintive meow and carried on with the leg rubbing just in case she might change her mind.

I don't know what got into me, Margaret thought as she put away her treats.

In the supermarket, she had overheard a lady tutting to her children about the 'three for the price of two' offer on mince pies.

Margaret had blurted out "I'll buy a box from you," before she'd had time to think.

The lady's son had frowned and said, "You can't buy it, if it's free," and Margaret's face had turned puce. Hot and bothered, she apologised and beetled off to find the pilchards.

"Quick, go and tell her," Margaret's hot ears had heard the lady say and the boy and his sister had skidded to a stop in front of her.

"Mum says you can have the extra box of mince pies because we don't need them."

The children were smiling at Margaret and the girl's bunches swung as she nodded her head, eyes wide with the importance of their message.

"Only thing is, you'll have to wait for us at the checkout because," the boy glanced at the lonely tin of pilchards in Margaret's wire basket, "We've got a lot more stuff than you."

"How kind. Thank your Mum. I don't mind waiting."

Margaret had to wait so long she began to feel embarrassed. The lady sent her children over again.

"Mum says you should sit down. There's a chair here, look." They showed her to a plastic chair and Margaret sat down.

"That's better," Margeret smiled at them.

The girl was gazing at Margaret's feet which were spilling over her shoes in folds of discomfort.

"Does that hurt?" The girl winced at Margaret with open concern.

"It's not too bad," Margaret told her, "It's better now I'm sitting down."

When the mother had finally bagged up and paid for her trolley load. She drove it towards Margaret. In addition to the mince pies, she insisted Margaret take the custard and box of chocolates too.

"No, you must," she said, beaming over the heads of her excited children, "Happy Christmas to you."

The mother drove her load towards the exit, the children turning to call Christmas greetings to Margaret as they danced off in her wake. Margaret got to her feet and watched them, those bunches swinging so happily, until they disappeared through the doors then she picked up her holdall of goodies and headed for the bus stop.

Once her Christmas fayre had been stowed, Margaret put some non-festive food in Tink's bowl and opened a tin of soup. Whilst the soup was heating, she let the cat out but he was tapping at the window to come back in again before she had finished eating. As she washed up bowl and pan, Margaret considered having a mince pie. It was, after all, Christmas Eve but decided, no, she would wait. The glow of anticipation was almost as good as the actual eating. Chores done, Margaret switched off the light and she and Tinks made their way towards the sitting room. By the door, Margaret took off her old gaberdine and hung it on the banister. The streetlight shone through the narrow, glazed panel of the front door just enough for her to find her pocket torch which was in its usual place on the sideboard. She opened the sitting room door and in they went. By the light of the torch, Margaret took from the cardboard box next to the side-table, the larger of the two wrapped figures. She unwrapped the delicate paper and there he was, the second shepherd, complete with crook and a lamb under his arm. The shepherd was set carefully down, next to the older shepherd with the chewed face, damage from Tinks's younger days. The shepherds' place was behind Joseph, on the other side of the manger to the 'kings from afar' bearing their important gifts. Margaret shone the torch around so each figure had their turn in the spotlight. She smiled gently at Mary and felt another warm glow at the thought of completing the nativity scene in the morning. Satisfied all was well in the stable, Margeret twiddled the knob of the television set. It took its usual time to warm up, then she twiddled the other knob until she found her programme and backed to the settee. Once seated, Margaret settled down with Tinks under the luxurious folds of their fur coat. The torch was extinguished until bedtime.

It hadn't always been this austere at Number 52 and to Margaret's mind, it shouldn't be now either. Elizabeth would have been most upset to know all that had happened. It had taken Margaret a long time to get used to calling her mother-in-law Elizabeth but it was true, they did end up more like sisters. They looked after each other in the years after Bob died, at least until Elizabeth got older, then their relationship evolved again, to that of nurse and patient. Elizabeth, having no other relatives, had always promised Margaret that she would inherit all her earthly possessions. She had shown her the will and told her who to call when the time came. As Elizabeth became less capable, it was Margaret who dealt with the bills. She was aware of electricity, rates and mortgage instalments coming out of Elizabeth's bank account. Elizabeth had told her that the house had cost eighteen thousand pounds when she and Bob's father had bought it.

"I'm sure we've paid back a lot more than that!" Elizabeth would declare, "But we'll be alright. Thank heaven, Teddy set up those life premium things and of course your contributions help Margaret. Every little helps!"

When the time came, things weren't quite so straightforward as Elizabeth had envisaged.

"No problem with the will," Mr Brent the solicitor told Margaret, "But there is the problem of the mortgage."

"Can't I just carry on paying it off as always?" Margaret's sensible remedy to the problem was met with sober headshaking.

It turned out that Margaret had to take out a new mortgage with the bank in her own name and attached to her own account. Despite the bank girl's earnest explanations, Margaret never understood why the outstanding mortgage of one thousand, five hundred pounds increased overnight to four thousand.

"We've done our research," the girl told her brightly, "And because you're so close to retirement age, we've arranged the monthly payments so you'll be finished on your retirement birthday. Phew!" The girl made a silly face and fanned it with her hand.

Margaret blinked at her.

"So," the girl wrapped it up with a smile, "Your monthly instalments will be two hundred pounds per month."

Margaret's felt her face drop. "But that's most of my wages," she stammered.

"I know," the girl turned sympathetic, then helpful, "If you can't manage and want to sell, I know an estate agent who would be happy to help you."

"I'll manage," Margaret's face was now set firm and after a few signatures, she was free to go.

And she had managed. The winter after Elizabeth went was miserable. Teddy's premium for when Elizabeth's time came had all been kept by the solicitor for funeral expenses and fees and Margaret had had to do some drastic belt-tightening. It had been hard but during the next summer, she had made her first acquaintance with serendipity.

Margaret had been walking past the scruffy, old charity shop when a tall, beautiful girl had come out shouting, "Fine! Don't then!"

The girl had dumped a binbag next to the bin by the bus stop and stomped off down the road. Spilling from the binbag, Margaret could see part of a sumptuous, silver-striped fur coat, like Gina Lollobrigida would wear or Sophia Loren. Margaret looked around but nobody seemed at all interested. Margaret picked up the bag and took it to the shop.

"I think there's been a mistake," she told the ladies.

"Oh no," they said, "We can't take that sort of thing anymore."

Disbelieving of her ears, Margaret looked from one to the other, "So, do you mean… can I keep it?"

The women looked down their noses at her but Margaret was used to that.

"Yes, you can have it," one of them said. She tucked the arm that was hanging out into the bag, "Be careful though," she cautioned Margaret, "People get very angry when they see this kind of thing these days." She looked at Margeret sternly, "Under no circumstances do you tell anyone that you got it from us. Is that clear?"

Margaret nodded, thanked them and quickly took the coat home. She'd have thought it would be heavy but it was ever so light. She left it in the bag and hurried to catch her bus. The best of it, she found out when she got back home, was at the bottom of the bag was a matching hat. Sometimes

Margaret wore it on her head, sometimes on her feet or sometimes Tinks curled up in it. It made a lovely nest for him.

Her other lucky find had been more recent. She'd got to the bus stop one morning and there on the bench was a giftset box of two miniature bottles of vintage port, one tawny, one ruby. There was a white card stuck to the box. It had 'Ace of Cups' and the number 52 written on it. Margaret glanced around but no one seemed to own it so she'd popped it into her holdall and zipped it up. She was reminded of Elizabeth. They used to enjoy their Christmas tipple. It had always been sherry in those days but Margaret was sure the port would be just as nice.

Christmas Day. Baby Jesus was in the manger. Margaret had watched Swan Lake on the television as she did every Christmas morning and eaten her 'heat up meal for one, turkey and gravy with potatoes and carrots.' She had heated up a mince pie at the same time and had a generous dollop of custard with it. Delicious.

Sitting in ample furry comfort amongst a few chocolate wrappers, Margaret raised her glass admiring the ruby liquid.

"Here's to you Bob. Cheers Elizabeth and Teddy too."

She took a little sip.

"Cheers Mum and Dad."

Margaret thought about her loved and lost ones, the boy and the little girl with her happily swinging hair bunches and wondered what Christmas might be like in that kind family. She began singing and humming half remembered carols, a pilchard replete Tinks purring away beside her.

Snow had fallen, Snow on Snow

Snow on Snow

In the bleak midwinter

Long, long, long ago.

The Food of Love

George Appleyard adored his wife. He loved her toothy grins, her kindness and that wholesomeness she had about her. Life with Hazel was easy and teasy and fun.

"You're such a bottom man, George," Hazel would tell him and it was true, those curves made him feel happy and content. Hazel had, in his view, the perfect bottom. It looked like a pair of well-grown watermelons in those green trousers she was wearing. The trousers were slightly shiny from wear and stretch. He knew they were a soft and comfy fit because he was wearing a similar pair himself. Hazel was weeding the strawberry patch, humming quietly. George had just got up from weeding around the potatoes and found his various aches assuaged by this wondrous vision.

They had met during the talent worship days of art college. Hazel had been in the canteen dreamily queuing beside her friend Ann when,

"Oi! You! Stop staring at my friend's bottom!"

Ann's reprimand had made Hazel jump. Turning her head, she had been surprised to meet eyes with a blushing George.

Two hearts had flipped.

"Sorry," George had grinned looking bashful, "Couldn't help it."

Ann had glowered, but Hazel had laughed before turning away.

It wasn't long before she and George were pleased to bump into each other again, soon seeking each other out and evolving into a cool couple, who kept each other grounded during the hedonistic days of student life.

Upon completion of three years of mosaics, daubing and unique pottery, they floundered into adulthood. Like so many budding artists, they soon had to resign themselves to the fact that money does matter. All that flair had to be set aside and George drove himself, a round peg, into the square hole of accountancy. Hazel, blessed with lovely teeth as well her rounder assets, became a dental nurse and living advert for the services expensively provided.

Sadly, the children they had assumed would arrive, did not, even after heroic efforts and the emotional helter-skelters of fertility treatment. They nursed each other through the disappointments, spoiling themselves with holidays and other luxuries which increasingly failed to satisfy. The often talked of dream was to abandon city life. Whilst gazing at a palm tree sunset over elaborate cocktails they didn't really want, the dream took shape. Why not put in an offer for that place they had always pointed out on visits to their favourite beach?

"I can go back to painting and you to clay," Hazel held George's hand, opening the fingers and cupping them to her cheek, "Where did my potter go?"

George was looking at her. They'd both become tetchy in London, bickering over nothing and even here didn't feel content or at ease.

She turned his hand, brushing his knuckle with a kiss, "Doesn't have to be fantastic. We can make it homely. Do our own thing. Imagine having the space to just be," she shrugged, her blue eyes searching his, "us."

George was thinking. George was nodding.

"Enough space. We can grow our own food. Self-sufficiency."

His face broke into a complicit grin. He raised his eyebrows twice, "Freedom!" and again the double eyebrow lift, "The Good Life!" George was beaming, "Why not?"

Flickers of hope and spontaneity were dancing between them.

"Sounds more like it."

"No more overtime."

"No more teeth."

"What are we waiting for?"

Neither voiced it, but as their family wasn't a growing one, onerously sought salaries were no longer essential.

The weekend after their return, they set off for their coast, feeling properly excited. The rickety 'For Sale' sign, bleached by years of sun was still standing. They knocked on doors and called out. No one responded so they had a look around, peering through windows, liking what they saw, unaware that they too were being observed and meeting with approval. After some tracking down of the agent and negotiations, the house and all that space became theirs. They made the house comfortable and began digging.

Their first harvest was not a success. The courgettes rotted, the beans expired, deer ate the carrot tops, slugs the lettuce and the wind blew the peas out of the ground. The potatoes were good though.

Over the winter they went to the beach and filled their trailer with rotting seaweed, which they dug into the soil together with manure from the nearby stables. Their efforts were rewarded, and the enriched earth became more inclined to produce. Hazel and George found they had learned much from that very best of teachers, the previous year's mistakes.

Another source of information came from their neighbour, tiny Mrs Meade. Hazel found her a bit creepy at first because she seemed to appear from nowhere. Often Mrs Meade brought them gifts, bunches of water cress, bags of juicy cherries or shiny chestnuts, as well as timely advice on this or that vegetable's requirements. They found the wizened lady a source of amusement, and Hazel would tease George that his admirer was back again. Mrs Meade would stand close under his chin, her blue eyes peering from under the red scarf that covered her yellowy, white ponytail as she dispatched the day's advice. She was so sweet and knowledgeable that they became fond of her. When Hazel mentioned it would be nice to have bees, Mrs Meade sourced two hives for them, and she told them where to buy bountiful hens. They bought six and a glorious rooster, who they decided to call Sir Fowler.

The next harvest was giddying. They stuffed themselves with their tender vegetables and dew fresh fruits. What wasn't munched raw was sauced or frozen, pickled, or turned into jam. The walls of the kitchen became imbued with aromas of drying herbs, spicy sauces and rich sweetness, carrying through and mingling with those of Hazel's oil paints in the adjacent room. The potter's wheel sat unused in the shed. George was just too busy to get round to it. They took turns to cook, treating each other to ever more delicious recipes, over which they clinked glasses, all twinkles and new dimples. Their physiques changed. Both tall, but formerly lanky, they became sturdy and bronzed. Physical labour made them honed and graceful. They found they smelt good.

During spring of the next year, Mrs Meade's visits became more frequent. She came with little poesies for Hazel or rare herbs for them to try. One day she brought strange stick structures which she nonchalantly placed around the garden.

"Come on, let's find out!" George pulled Hazel up and they went over, smiling and bemused.

"What are these then Mrs Meade?" George asked in his cheerful way.

Hazel's heart swelled at his wonderful niceness, and they waited for Mrs Meade to finish what she was doing. She was bent over, her knobbly hands carefully placing another stick figure against the fuchsia. When it was arranged to her satisfaction, she straightened up and greeted them with a smile so big that all her wrinkles became one.

"They are for Alban Hefin." Her cloudy eyes took in their mystified faces and she chuckled, "You'd know it as the summer solstice. The crowning of the King of Summer. Such a night!" She closed her eyes at the divine thought of it. Then she opened them wide and her strange, high voice turned serious. "They have to stay." She looked anxiously from George to Hazel. "You won't move them, will you?" Then smiling at their earnestly shaking heads, "You see, I'm putting them here for you two. They're for you!"

She turned her attention back to the figures and studied them then nodded and bade George and Hazel good afternoon.

They watched until she disappeared around the house then their eyes met in wary amusement.

"What was all that about?" George asked.

"What was it she said, 'Alban Hefin?' Come on, let's look it up."

They went into the house. Hazel found the answer first.

"Oh!" she said, glancing up "Looks like our Mrs Meade is a druid!"

"Well, we'd better not move her effigies then. Remember that film?"

Hazel snorted, "The Wicker Man? Hardly George. Mrs Meade loves us. Specially you."

She opened her eyes wide. "If we did move them, what do you think would happen?"

George gave an admonishing look. "We just don't want to upset her, do we?"

Hazel couldn't help smiling at his serious face, "Don't worry, I won't move her things." She couldn't quite bring herself to say effigies. "Anyway, I think they're rather charming."

The next day was warm and clear. Mrs Meade came round late afternoon. "It's good we have fine weather," she told them, "Aine will be pleased." Her face turned fearful. "She can be vengeful you know." Her eyes flashed towards the figures and back at a now solemn George and Hazel. With a sigh of relief that nothing had been disturbed, Mrs Meade gave them a quick smile then took from her basket a piece of cardboard whose sides had been folded to make a small punnet. The punnet, which contained several tiny mushrooms, she presented to George.

He raised his eyebrows, "What are these Mrs Meade?"

"Oh, they're good," she told them. "You must eat them today, while they're fresh. Just sprinkle them on your dinner as they are. So very good for you."

Hazel had made herby pea and goats cheese risotto for supper. They eyed the punnet between them on the table.

George had a gleam in his eye. "Are these what I think they are?"

Student day visions wafted between them.

"Oh, come on George!" In an impulsive move, Hazel divided the contents of the punnet between their plates. "Bon Appetit! Cheers to Alban Hefin!"

They clinked glasses and began their meal under the evening sky. The mushrooms didn't have much taste at all.

A little later, it occurred to Hazel that George's head was so very like a beautiful pumpkin. Strange she hadn't noticed that before. He was such a handsome pumpkin that she had to kiss him.

George, enraptured by Hazel's luscious leek features, was delighted when her flat bean fingers began caressing him and pulling him towards her.

She marvelled at the strength of his marrow arms. Such dark green stripes.

George spread his courgette fingers. How he relished taking hold of those wondrous watermelons. From ample pomegranates, George's spellbound gaze travelled down and with infinite gentleness, he parted leaves to find the deep, dark moistness of the fig beneath.

Hazel gasped pushing him gently away. She gazed at his face and then was further amazed as George transformed before her very eyes.

Who was this tall, stern being wearing a crown of candles, gazing down at her with the flashing arrogance of a sun god? Hazel leapt up and fled, her limbs elongating as she moved. George watched this new Hazel, long hair streaming with ivy and cobwebs. Her flight only served to arouse him further and he chased. Glancing over her shoulder, Hazel saw the magnificent form dashing after her, candles swaying but somehow still alight. Run and be chased. Why, of course we must run. They cavorted around under the luminous sky until he finally caught her. Once in his arms, Hazel was smitten by his power and magnetic heat. Her sun god was a passionate lover.

They were awoken early on Midsummers Day by the loud crowing of a closely observing Sir Fowler. Surprised at finding themselves in the garden and covered by a blanket of the softest wool, they'd never seen before, they sat up. Cocooning themselves, they gazed at each other.

"That was quite a night." George said softly.

 Hazel, relieved that he looked like her George again, patted his hair back into place.

"I know," she said, a twinkle of surprise lighting up her eyes.

Birds sang in the day as they rested close, watching the sun paint pink the windows of their luxurious henhouse. King and queen no longer, just garden creatures like the others scurrying and fluttering around.

Mrs Meade never visited again. Maybe it was a lingering effect of the mushrooms but George and Hazel didn't feel surprised or concerned by her disappearance. They kept to their word and the stick figures remained in the garden until one spring morning, they weren't there anymore. The wind and rain had gradually dismantled them and they had been taken back into the earth. George and Hazel weren't even sure when they had gone, they were so happily busy and tired these days, what with the garden and their darling twins, Emrys and Willow.

To Leave The Cupboard

1

The cupboard was my mother's punishment for me, for my wickedness. For, as she told me many times, I am a witch. My punishment was frequent and became predictable but unavoidable. For several days before, the constant irritability provoked by my presence, would turn to mounting intolerance. Rarely, I had committed a misdemeanour, other times I would have been trying to demonstrate my goodness. I learned to avoid her, trying to prevent the snapping point. How I dreaded the look on her face as she whirled towards me, skirts hitched up at the sides. That look made my body stop working but not my senses. Always that smell, the smell of deep, dark, iron blood. Before I could think to flee, I would be grabbed and hauled down the corridor. Now, too late, my body started working again. I would struggle and beg,

"No Mother, please no!"

Faced with the cupboard, I would be pinned against her taut, corseted body, while the door swung open, yawning out its musty insides.

"Get in!"

Grunting with the effort, pushing, slapping, kicking, she would shove me into the darkness and I would crash through cobwebs until I slammed against the back wall. Old plaster sprinkled, daylight disappeared, the door slammed shut, the bolt slammed in.

"Evil little witch!"

Ripping clinging webs from my face, my panicked screams would turn to sobs and pleas then whimpers. Exhausted, I would draw my dress around me to keep the things that crept and crawled out of my clothes and pray for release. I would rock myself for comfort. I would rock myself for hours.

The cupboard was under the back stairs and followed the angle of their turn. It was highest close to the door and went down with the stairs. The floor was earth, unlike the rest of the house, which had tiled or wooden floors. The earth was a jumble of rags, old shoes, bottles and broken tools. And dust, old, old dust. It was quite dark but once my eyes became accustomed, I could make out my surroundings. On sunny days light poured in from the high barred windows at this end of the corridor and filtered through cracks and holes in the wooden stairs. Those were the good days. Dull days, winter days, I could barely make out my hands in front of my face. It was dry apart from my tears. I was not alone. The stringy-legged, bulbous-bodied spiders glared at me with their many eyes as they carried their precious egg bundles to a safer, darker corner. At first, the sight of them made me curl into a ball of screaming terror but I got used to them. I did get used to being in the cupboard. I was in there so much that watching them go about their business became a source of fascination. Once, for something to do, I poked my head around the turn of the cupboard to try to see what was down in the sloping end. Something soft and strange felt my neck, making me scream and jump back. When I recovered, I peered at the creature. It was a bat. In the gloom I could see it's strange little face. It had a long grey beard. It didn't move, not like the bats in the attic, who flitted about when disturbed. It was just hanging there forever. I moved away, tried to erase the vision.

"Please, oh please let me out."

Occasionally, steps would come down the corridor and I would hold my breath. I got to know the various footsteps, Marie the maid, was light, she would run up and down the staircase as quickly and quietly as she could; the housekeeper, paced steady and respectful and Marcel who would stomp up and down the stairs, banging dust down on me. Father never came near. It wasn't his part of the house. This staircase led to the servants' room, which had two small beds, a chest of drawers upon which stood a candle holder, a jug, washbasin and two brushes. Two rosaries. They had a chair each and there was a wardrobe with a small mirror. They didn't have many clothes. It was very neat. I liked being in there. It was sparse but cosy and it smelt nice.

Across the corridor was the storeroom where fruit was kept good on big trays, onions hung, and meats cured. In the middle of the of the floor a deep, black stain spread out beneath a sturdy ceiling hook where the pig side hung, for the ham. At the end of the corridor, a door led into the big sooty attic, warm in summer, cold in winter. There were things in there to look at and trunks to open. It was a place for games waiting to be played.

My mother's grinding footsteps would always make me sit up, heart pounding at the swish of dress and steady clip of boot on tile. They would stop in front of the door, and I would feel sick with dread and hope. If I made a sound, she would give a little sniff,

"Clearly, you haven't learnt your lesson yet!"

She would turn on her heel and the swish and clip would retreat again. I learned not to make a sound. Sometimes, she would pause and change her mind anyway and I would go back to my silent pleas and rocking. But she always came back eventually. Alerted and thirsty, I would prepare myself as the bolt slid and the door swung open. Light! But light framing my mother's imposing frame. Our eyes would meet. I never knew if I could go or must stay and this too was wrong. She took my indecision for insolence and would pull me out by ear or wrist.

"Well get out then!" she would hiss. "And get out of my sight, with your damnation eyes!

A slap would send me running down the corridor. I would go to the kitchen and drink at last and eat the food laid out for me by Marie or the housekeeper at a little table in the corner. Often, they would be in the kitchen preparing food or cleaning. I liked watching them, but they didn't talk to me. They were afraid of me and tried not to see me because I am a witch.

In fine weather, I would escape to the garden. I loved being outside. The front garden was formal and clipped, with wrought iron fence and gates. The back was larger, with fruit trees against one wall, lawns, made unruly with flower beds but disciplined by a vegetable garden towards the back wall. There was a gate leading to the park and fields but I didn't venture there. The gardens were maintained by a man who came during the week. He didn't live in the house. He lived in a cottage in the park. He didn't speak to me either. My favourite place was a seat against the wall hidden by a spreading, dancing rose. I recovered in the embrace of the sun basked stone, cheered by the cheeky robin and the blackbird's joyful song, refreshed by the scent of the lilac roses. If it was raining, I would lurk in the house trying to be invisible and learn things by unseen observation.

2

I had a brother, but he was good. Marcel, blonde and podgy in his sailor suit. When he was little Marcel was allowed to touch Mother. His big, blue eyes would gaze up at her, as he tugged her dress and she would smile and lift him to her lap. She would talk gently to him and kiss his soft skin.

"Blonde, like your father," Mother would say gently pulling a soft curl and smiling as it bounced up from her fingers. If she caught me watching, her eyes would turn hard and she would send me from the room. I never knew why I was a witch, what I had done to deserve these cursed eyes. It was a mystery I puzzled over and over.

On days too cold to be outside, I would sneak into the parlour with them and be mesmerised by the fire crackling in the grate as I listened.

"When you're grown up," she would tell him, "You're going to be a rich merchant. Marcel is going to be important."

She and Marcel would nod at each other, her smiling, he solemn, "And you're going to marry a beautiful wife and live in a beautiful house in a town. A fine house with proper servants," More nodding, "And you'll invite your Maman to stay, won't you?" Nod, nod. "Maman would like that."

I used to wonder about my prospects. They were never discussed. Witches don't have any.

I was dark haired, like Mother, but mine was nearly black and I had paler face and skinny bones. Mother had large hazel eyes, not like my black, witchy eyes. She made Marcel's clothes herself, with pride. They were fine and soft. What she said was true, he did look like a prince of angels in them. My dresses were made by the housekeeper. They were made from the course, grey material of her old dresses, even the pinafore. Mother wore dark blue dresses in winter, pale blue in summer and of a lighter fabric. The lace collar and cuffs were cream in winter and white in summer and of intricate design.

Father wasn't tall but he was a big man, with a large, red nose protruding out from his whiskered face. He never spoke to me. If he caught sight of me, he would glare and snarl and I would run to hide. I tried to keep out of his way. He was mostly upstairs or out on his horse with the farm manager. At mealtimes I heard Mother and Father talking in the dining room but they didn't say very much.

Mother could be kind. When the cat had kittens and they were weaned, I watched Mother take food out for them. They usually died anyway. I supposed it was because their mother was just a tiny cat herself. It was such a sad sight, watching them writhe around dying. Mother didn't like me to see that. When she turned and saw that I was looking, she would shout at me.

"Get away, you stupid child! Do you want to catch their diseases?"

The next time I went back, the little bodies were gone.

3

Occasionally there would be great preparations which meant that people were coming to dine. The planning would start a few days before along with the mounting excitement. On the day, everyone except Father would be up very early. The gardener who had been summonsed the week before would deliver armfuls of flowers which Mother herself would put into vases set with water by the maid in the corridor, parlour and dining room. Mimosa, lilacs, lilies, depending on the season and always roses. I remember their scents and how they made the house beautiful. Mother would come into the kitchen and fuss and chide the perspiring housekeeper and red-faced Marie. Nothing was ever quite right and they would puff out their cheeks in relief when she left to fuss elsewhere.

"What else can be expected of peasants?" she would demand on her way out.

The dining room had been made beautiful with shining glasses and silverware. I would wander around watching all the activity, my stomach growling at the aromas of roasting meat and bubbling soup. The cooking seemed to be going very well to me.

As the carriages arrived, I would be in my place behind the rhododendron bush to watch and see. It was mostly men alone but some came with their wives. I liked looking at their dresses and jewellery and how they did their hair but they weren't as pretty as Mother and always looked stiff and sniffy.

When they had gone Mother would go to bed and cry. Father would stay at table drinking the wine. Sometimes he fell asleep in his chair and once I stole over to get a proper look at him. Suddenly a red thread blue eye popped open and then another. He drew himself up roaring and threw out his arm to catch hold of me. I yelped and too quick for him ran to hide.

Next day, before the cupboard, my eyes were held by those of my mother's.

She shook me like the terrier a rat, "You want to make us destitute?" Slap, "Never," Slap, "Ever," Slap, "Let that man see you again."

And then she shoved me in.

4

One of the times I did do something which even to my mind could be seen to deserve punishment was to do with Marcel. We weren't supposed to talk to each other but when he was little we used to play secret games anyway. It started off as peek a boo. How I loved hearing him chortle as I peeped at him from my hands. When he started walking, I would hold his chubby hands as he bounced on the beds laughing and shouting, "Faster, faster!" and I let him win at tig in the garden. We had our imaginary friends in the mirror, his was Bernard, mine was Isabelle and we would talk to them, exchanging information about our different worlds. They would try to entice us in through the magic mirror-gate but Marcel and I agreed that this was something we must never do for if we did, they would never let us back. Hide and seek or exploring the attic, we had a lot of fun in that big, old house. I will always hear the happy sounds of Marcel's laughter brightly echoing through the rooms but it is always followed by his haunting screams. I wonder what happened to him.

A gruff old man used to come to the house to teach him reading, writing and arithmetic. It was about that time that Marcel stopped liking me. It was as if he, like everyone else, stopped seeing me. I followed him around, trying to coax him to talk and play with me again but he wouldn't. I had to content myself with the cat. She was only allowed in the house to keep the mice out and was so thin you could see all her ribs. Sometimes I shared my food with her so we became friends but it wasn't the same.

One day I followed Marcel into his bedroom and tried to peep at the book he was reading out loud. He didn't notice at first but then must have felt my breath on his neck. He turned in a fury and hit me with the book.

"Get out!" he shouted. "You're not allowed in here."

"Why not?" I shouted back. "Why are you being so mean to me Marcel? And why do you have this nice room with books?"

He stared at his book. He was breathing hard, like Mother before an outburst.

Loneliness made me desperate, "Why don't you like me anymore?" I had to know what I had done.

His answer was to grab my hand and sink his teeth into it. I couldn't believe he was doing that. He bit harder and harder. I watched his teeth sinking in and in. Then my other hand punched him in the eye. That was just when Mother came in. I tried to show her the bite mark on my hand but that was of no consequence. Her wrath at witnessing my injury of Marcel was overwhelming. I was slapped and heaved, legs whirling and bumping, down the big staircase, along the corridor and inside the cupboard before even the blood ran. Marcel had a black eye, but it didn't last nearly as long as his bite mark. We never spoke again.

5

My favourite time was Sunday morning. Everyone went to church, except me. Witches aren't allowed. Our house was quite a distance from the nearest village, something my mother found insupportable, but it was good for me. It meant that on Sundays, I had the chance to explore the whole house. Lured by enticing aromas, I always started in the kitchen. Sniffing the cooking meat, I would peep under cloths and poke my finger into stewed fruit and suck the sweetness that witches aren't usually allowed. Then I would wander from room to room, caressing bedspreads, peeping in drawers and little boxes on Mother's dressing table. How her brooches sparkled in the light. I would open the big armoire and look at her dresses, laying my face against them, imagining her looking down on me with the same soft eyes, stroking my head with the same loving hands as she did with Marcel.

In Marcel's room, I would play with his toys and look hard at his books with their colourful pictures and the letters I could never understand. I felt strange in Father's bedroom. It was quite uninteresting apart from some strange things in his drawers, for which I couldn't work out a purpose. It didn't smell very nice. I didn't spend much time in there. I liked his study though. There were bigger books than those in Marcel's. One had a gold paint in the writing and in the pictures, which showed of bearded men in long robes, and beautiful and terrible things. I spent many hours gazing at the pictures in this book.

In the dining room was a tall clock with a gold face and a big gold pendulum. It rang out at different times and could be heard all over the house. This was very useful to me. I knew my numbers from listening to Marcel's lessons. Twelve strikes meant that I should put things carefully back in their place, go downstairs and tuck myself away again. The carriage would soon return.

My bedroom was downstairs. A little room next to the cupboard with the kitchen opposite which meant it was usually warm and had smells to make your stomach rumble all night long. It had a small high window that would have looked out on to the side path if I had been very tall to see out of it. I could see the stars and sometimes the moon through it. I didn't sleep all night and drew imaginary images in the air and made up stories in my head. Sometimes on bright moon nights I would wander around the house. I liked to sit at the table imagining I was wearing a gold dress surrounded by sumptuous tableware and glorious food. Everyone was polite and deferred to me. If anyone looked down their nose at Mother or displeased me in any way, I would order Mother to take them to the cupboard and lock them in there for a week.

Another game could be played when the moon shone in through the circular window above the front or the back door, lighting up a path on the tiles of the main corridor. This became my vessel as seen in the book of gold. The dark tiles were the water and I had to keep carefully on board as I sailed for if I fell I would surely drown or be caught by the serpents who raised themselves up to try to catch me.

Sometimes as I was playing, strange noises came from upstairs. Creaking and moaning as if there were ghosts at play. Sometimes Father would cross from his room to Mother's his white gown and moustache lit up by the candle in its holder and I would quickly slip back to mine and hide under my blankets before they found me out. Mother always looked pale and watery the days after those nights.

6

Our father became ill. I overheard the housekeeper telling Marie that the pains were worsening, and he was turning grey. The doctor came, his horse waiting patiently for him at the gate, while he tried to make Father better. I heard the groaning. Mother spent many hours in Father's room, trying to feed him soup and medicine. Father's hacking and retching didn't stop all night long, but then it lessened and I had hope. The noises ceased altogether but the housekeeper and Marie were still grave and a few days later, the housekeeper told Marie that Father was dead. Mother wore a black dress and looked more stony-faced than ever. Even chubby Marcel looked troubled. I shrank like the tiniest mouse. Men came and took Father away in a box. Everyone but me went to church on a Thursday.

People came to the house to offer their condolences. The advocate and the doctor were invited in. Mother, steely formidable in her grief, put up with the advocate's circuitous explanations. The doctor, who arrived with a hopeful air, left despondent, his wheedling enquiries having been met with firm disdain. Others were kept politely at the door.

"Madame is too distraught to receive you," the housekeeper kept saying and noses, sincere or sniffy were jerked back. Well-meant words would have to be passed on via the domestic staff. Heads bowed graciously and the visitors returned to their homes on foot, horse or in carriages.

Life in the house went on without Father. The routine didn't much change. Not at first. It was better for me as Mother spent her days in Father's study. Occasionally the advocate would call to offer advice and the still hopeful doctor would be allowed in for ever briefer liaisons. Life went on like this from winter to summer then one day Mother went out for the day in the carriage. Two weeks later a carriage drew up and several packages were delivered and put in Mother's room. The next day Mother was in her room all day apart from mealtimes. The day after that, mouths dropped open as she came down wearing a rustling dress of rose pink with cream lace, pink ribbon, pearls. Her expression forbade comment. Mouths snapped closed and downcast eyes disappeared out of her way.

7

Now that the mourning had officially come to an end, Mother went out in the carriage once then twice a week. At first Marcel went with her but after a while he had to stay home to study with a new tutor and she went off alone. Marcel grew bigger than me. His features changed. He looked more and more like Father. Poor Marcel. Mother stopped loving him. Her warm regard changed to cold and there were no more soft words and touches. I wondered whether perhaps there was a time when Mother had loved me as she had Marcel and then stopped. I didn't think so. I couldn't remember or even imagine it. I decided it must have been worse for Marcel - to once have been so adored and then not at all. At least he never got locked in the cupboard but Marcel was soon to endure another sort of punishment.

This tutor, Monsieur Picketty, couldn't have been more different to the kindly gentleman who had been his predecessor. His duty, he announced in quiet, menacing tones, was to prepare Marcel for school. I tried to listen, but the classroom door was firmly closed. Even with my ear pressed against the wood panelling of the next room, I couldn't hear enough to learn. Monsieur Picketty was very strict. He had a whip. If Marcel wasn't trying hard enough, he whipped him. I was turned to heart stop stone the first time I heard the slice of whip and Marcel shriek in shock and pain. I was peeping through the window once and I saw him do it. He made Marcel take his breeches down and lean over a chair and then whipped his nakedness six wicked times. I felt my brother's pain. I didn't know what to do. I thought about telling Mother, but she must have heard Marcel's cries. Why didn't she do something? Once I heard the rustle of her dress downstairs while Marcel was being punished. I went and looked right at her. Her eyes met mine

"He has to learn," was all she said.

She looked through me as if I was nothing at all.

8

One warm autumn day something happened, which I will never forget. I was in the front garden, trying to reach some blackberries that were crawling in between the railings, when a man walked in through the gate. He was limping, but had a strong, straight back. He caught sight of me and came close. I should have run away, but he was gazing at me with such intensity, that I was held there.

"Good day to you, Mademoiselle."

He had a nice voice and smiled but, strangely, he looked a bit afraid, so I smiled back.

"Good day to you too, Sir."

My voice surprised me. It rang loud and clear.

From under the dark forelock, a scar ran across his face, livid against his pale skin. I wondered what had happened to him. He glanced at the front door and cleared his throat.

"Might I find the lady of the house at home?"

He asked the question, as if it was of great importance and his eyes burned as if pain and tears were close.

I nodded that she was.

"Thank you."

He smiled at me. As he smiled, his eyes twinkled, and I felt mine twinkle back. It was such a lovely feeling that I would have liked to have smiled at him forever. It seemed to me he felt that too. He nodded still smiling, then turned and marched to the front door as if trying to hide his limp. The housekeeper opened it and he quietly asked if he could talk to Mother. I heard his name. He was called Jean-Vincent Valentin.

The housekeeper pushed the door closed. The man turned and smiled at me again, he looked uncertain then turned back and stared at the door. It opened but only a fraction. I couldn't hear what was said but the man's shoulders slumped. The door shut. He started limping to the gate then turned and came towards me.

"I didn't know," he said. Then, turning to the house, he called loudly, "I'm truly sorry, but I didn't know. How could I know?"

He stared at the door a moment longer then turned, head bowed and limped quickly away.

I was still staring at the gate through which the man had disappeared, when I heard the front door swing wide open. I turned and saw Mother and I could see that she was in a rage.

"Come here now!"

The words snarled out through grinding teeth and I knew what would happen. My feet obeyed and took my hammering heart towards her.

"What do you think you're doing?" Bang, thump, smack. "How dare you?" Slap, slap. "You know you're not allowed out here."

She dragged me in, hitting me on my head, face, shoulder, anywhere she could reach. She couldn't stop hitting.

I curled up on the floor and heard a cane being pulled out of the umbrella stand. I heard the cane in Mother's hand thwack down on me, I don't know how many times. Strangely, I didn't feel it much. My arms around my head, I lay there waiting for it to be over. The cane got thrown, clattering to the floor.

"Get her out of my sight!" Mother snarled and swish-clipped away in her stylish new boots.

Steady and light footsteps approached. The housekeeper and Marie helped me up and half carried, half dragged me to my bed. They looked after me and secretively were very kind to me after that day. They weren't afraid of me anymore. Perhaps they thought my wickedness had been beaten out.

9

Mother began to entertain regularly. These visitors were not like the people who used to come. The women wore clothes of beautiful colours and chattered and tittered like magpies and jays. The men were dashing and light of heart and laughter. Mother's face changed. She became pretty and gay. Her wardrobe bulged with new clothes of brightly coloured materials and ornamentation. She changed her hair. She changed her walk. When the visitors were in the house, I even heard her laugh.

In the kitchen, the housekeeper and Marie whispered about a fancy man and exchanged looks with raised eyebrows.

Mother went out more and more and when she was home, she shut herself in Father's study. My life became good. The housekeeper always let me have jam with my bread these days and cake and dessert. She and Marie would give me friendly squeezes and little pats. One day the housekeeper, who I was now allowed to call Alice, as long as Mother was not present, tucked me under my chin,

"I'm going to have to make you some new dresses young lady," she told me, "You're filling out at last."

A few days later, she gave me two new dresses. The material was the same but, as I unfolded them, I saw that the pinafores had flounces and pockets and there were flowers embroidered in white and red. They were the prettiest things I had ever owned.

"It was Marie who did the embroidery." Alice told me and Marie did a little curtesy. I couldn't stop thanking them and they smiled and smiled. Their eyes were very shiny.

"Can I wear one now?" I asked.

They both nodded and I ran to change. I felt as flouncy as my pinafore as I walked back into that kitchen. I couldn't stop straightening my flounces and touching those threaded flowers, soaking up the compliments from my two new friends. Whilst Mother and Marcel were in the dining room, I stole upstairs and looked at my reflection in the mirror in mother's room and found that I even looked quite pretty.

10

One morning bags appeared at the bottom of the stairs and Marcel and his bags were sent away to school. He looked nervous. Mother went out with him to the carriage. She spoke brief words and waved him away then returned to the house alone. Even though we hadn't been allowed to talk to each other, the house seemed strange without Marcel. There were stranger things to come.

Alice began looking as grave as when Father was ill. One October morning, she had to tell the man who came to do the garden that he wasn't to come anymore. He nodded and mumbled then went away, his tools hitched over his shoulder. More bags and boxes appeared at the bottom of the stairs and were collected by a much finer carriage than ours. The next day Alice had to send Marie away. Alice and I sat on her bed with our arms around her, trying to sooth her sobbing. I couldn't stop crying either. Alice helped put her few things in a bag. My new friend, Marie, left with red eyes as the dining room clock struck two.

To my horrified disbelief, the day after that it was Alice who was leaving. She had been very quiet whilst preparing food in the morning. I had thought it was because, like me, she was missing Marie. After serving lunch to Mother and clearing away, she took me to the pantry and showed me two covered plates hidden behind a sack of flour.

 "These ones are yours," She said, "Now you keep yourself scarce until you hear the clock strike five and then you eat your meal at your little table here in the kitchen, like you always do."

She bustled quickly out. I stood like a statue, happiness pouring out of my feet. When Alice came back to the kitchen, her face was as buttoned up as her coat. The corners of my mouth kept pulling down, like the pictures of a clown in one of Marcel's books.

I ran to her, "Don't leave Alice. Please don't leave me here." Alice hugged me very tight for a long moment then pulled my arms from around her big waist and held me away from her. Tears ran down her cheeks and her voice wobbled.

"It's not what I want, but we have to do as we're told."

Her voice became strong, "Now, you must know Grace that you are not a witch."

She shook her head, "That was just your Mother's nonsense but she's happier now and you are going to have a new life together in the town. Now you be a good girl and here," she gave me a little tinkling package tied up with string. "Here, you open this and know, whenever you hear it that Marie and I are thinking about you."

Her hands moved up to my face and she bent down and gave me a fierce kiss on my forehead. Then she turned and walked out of the kitchen. I heard her and Mother exchange stiff goodbyes and the front door open and close. Pain sliced through my heart.

I slipped out of the back door and hid behind the roses. There were no blooms at this time but sprays of bright red hips instead. In case Mother came looking for me, I opened the parcel straight away. It was a little grey cat, made out of the same material as my dresses. It had white eyes and whiskers, a red nose and a tiny little bell at its throat, which made the pretty tinkling sound. I held my little cat to my cheek and thought about all the things that had happened lately and what Alice had just told me.

"Not a witch,"

I tried not think about how it might be with only Mother and me in this house or in a new house in town. I couldn't imagine it.

11

I didn't see Mother for the rest of the day. It got cold outside towards dusk. I went in, listening hard. The kitchen was mean and gloomy. I lit a candle from the dwindling fire and put some logs on from the pile. The embers smoked then cheered and began licking round the dry wood, easing the awful quiet with pops and whistles. Alice's instructions stayed in my ears. I fetched my plates and ate my food, ears and eyes alert, but she stayed upstairs. I tidied away as I had watched Alice and Marie do so often, then I went to my room and played with my cat in the darkness till sleep came.

When I went into the kitchen the next morning, the fire was lively and I was shocked to see Mother already up and in there. I was about to dash back out but she smiled brightly and told me to come and eat up the breakfast she had laid out for me. I tucked my cat into my sleeve, hoping she wouldn't hear her tinkles and sat before the plate with its thick slices of bread. Unexpectedly the bread was laden with jam.

It's hard to eat when you're scared, especially if the bread is a little stale and you're being watched by the person who scares you. The unaccustomed smiling didn't help. It was strange and grim and fixed.

Mother had often called me sly, "A sly witch", and indeed my upbringing had taught me to be that. After watching my loud swallowing for a while, surely her eyes would be drawn to the window. Surely, she would stare out for a few seconds. Time enough for me to pluck the rest of the bread from my plate and stuff it in my pocket but I didn't want jam on my pretty dress. The painful munch swallowing went on. The bread didn't taste nice.

Suddenly she couldn't stand it, "Enjoy your breakfast," she said, with the same bright smile, "Don't forget to drink your milk.

I listened with relief as her footsteps went down the corridor, but she didn't go upstairs as I had expected. This meant she could come back at any time. I licked the jam off the bread then quickly stuffed it in my pocket. Just in time because, a moment later, she clipped back in. There was no way I could have eaten so much bread in that short time. We watched each other as I pretended to chew and swallow noisily. It worked. She was nodding approvingly at my plate. Then she nodded at the cup.

"And the milk," she said, "Don't forget your milk."

I picked up the cup and drank some of the milk. It tasted strange. It had the same taste as the bread but at least it was easier to swallow. To please Mother, to get the ordeal over with, I drank it all. She smiled at me again but then her face went all wobbly. I suddenly felt very sick and couldn't breathe hard enough, my swimming head fell on the plate with a heavy, unreal thud.

12

I awoke from the deepest sleep with a racing heart. My head hurt. I was sick. I was very thirsty and so cold. Things were digging into me and I realised that I was not in my bed. It was very dark, I shifted and tried to sit up. There was a reassuring tinkling at my sleeve as I pulled myself up and lent against the wooden door. The smell of dust, the earth beneath my fingers, sticky, hair-thin strings on my face, these things told me where I was. But why or how I was there, I couldn't work out. All I knew was that I was in the cupboard in the pitch dark and it was very, very quiet. There were no kitchen smells, no smoky warmth. The clock struck three. I pulled my little cat out of my sleeve and held her to my cheek. She tinkled and caught my tears.

I dozed and woke shivering, cuddled my aching stomach and dozed again. When next I stirred, the autumn day had begun outside and some light filtered into the cupboard. I waited and listened and tried to work out why I was in there. The last thing I remembered was Mother smiling at me. I played with my cat and thought of names for her. In the end, I called her Rose, because of the place where I first saw her. I wondered whether Marie had reached her family's home yet and Alice, her sister's. I thought about Marcel in his school. The clock struck three. I wondered what my mother was doing. I thought of all the bags in the hall and a horrible feeling crawled into me. Surely, surely, Mother wouldn't have forgotten me in here. Surely not. I stood up, as best I could in the cupboard and began calling for Mother. I called and called then listened hard. Not a sound. I screamed for Mother at the top of my voice. I screamed for help. I banged on the door with a broken tool and screamed for anyone. I screamed and screamed until my voice ran out. Exhausted, I sank to the floor and felt around for Rose. She tinkled and cuddled against my face, reminding me of Alice and Marie. It was pitch dark now. The clock struck eight.

When I next opened my eyes, my throat was raw and I felt weak and weary, but it must have been a bright, clear day outside because there was more light to see with. I rummaged around and found a heavy, smooth piece of thin metal. I tried sliding it through the edge of the door, but I couldn't get it to even touch the bolt, so I gave up on the door. I crawled round and worried the wood trying to force the cracks to break. I found different tools and tried to make the holes bigger. In desperation, I shoved the rubbish to the sides, lay down under the lower stairs and tried forcing the wood off with my feet. I kicked and forced and scraped that wood but nothing, apart from a few splinters, gave way. I heaved myself back to the door and knelt up. I knew Mother had gone, that the house was empty but maybe a chance passer-by would hear. I shouted and called for as long as I could, but my voice was tired and feeble and before long I knew the sounds that I could muster weren't loud enough for anyone to hear. So, I lay down with Rose by my face and watched the dust motes in the shafts of light. They were pretty and so many.

Time, day and night, I lost all sense of them. Rose fell from my hand and I was too tired to find her. Everything hurt, my head, my eyes, my insides were twisting and knotting. I writhed in pain. Oh, how I suffered and slept and woke and suffered anew. And then quite suddenly, I escaped. I simply drifted out. I looked with compassion at the poor girl, in the embroidered pinafore, lying on her bed of rubbish. She struggled on, Rose by her side, but I was free. The cupboard door was no longer a barrier. I passed right through it.

It was strange seeing the house this way. I floated above the uneven tiles of the corridor into the dining room and bid the clock good day. The big, gold pendulum swung, reassuring and reliable. I noticed the remains of Mother's evening meal on the table. Sensing her presence, I left, passing through the day room across the east, west corridor to the other rooms that were never used. Bright rays pierced through the closed shutters. The sparse furniture was furry with dust and spiders reigned over this domain. One room, at the back of the house, had arches and a strange cupboard with little seats and a grill. There was a higher table with tarnished candle holders and on the wall, a picture of a man with a flowing beard. This reminded me of Father's study, and I went up there. I was astonished by the disarray. I went up to the attic. It wasn't so much fun as it used to be when I could discover the hidden treasures in the chests and under dust sheets. I studied the bats instead. They were all cuddled up in a corner, leather wings wrapped tight around their bodies. I found them sweet to watch, but my presence disturbed them, so I drifted into Alice and Marie's room and felt the warmth of their kind spirits.

A tinkling sent me rushing me down to the girl in the cupboard. Poor thing, her cheeks were sunk right in and with every breath she gave a little moan. I stayed with her and talked of all the people who had loved her and the happy times watching baby Marcel, and amongst the roses and the books. We felt the presence of our friends and that included Jean-Vincent Valentin with his twinkling smile. After many hours, the moaning lessened and then it ceased. The clock struck three. That was the last time I heard it strike for a very, long time. I stayed in the cupboard. I wanted to now.

13

After I don't know how long, I felt I should do something for the little, dead girl. I wanted to cover her in lilac rose petals and drifted out to the garden. But what a change! The garden was covered in great mounds of brambles. They sprawled over everything, swamping the flower beds and vegetables and rambling up the trees. It was the same in the front garden, the few cheeky sprays had turned into a monster bush, scrambling up the shutters and strangling the railings. I returned to the back garden to seek out my roses. They were struggling for light amongst their powerful cousins, but of course, I couldn't pick the few blooms anyway. I went up to watch the bats. It was spring and the mother bats kept together in a separate place to the main group and took turns to go out at night so there was always some bats to look after the babies and keep them warm. When the baby bats started flying outside, I went with them and watched them learn.

When the winters came and the bats stayed in, I did a lot of thinking. I thought about Mother. She hadn't forgotten me in the cupboard. Those sudden smiles would never have been for me. She had deliberately locked me in and left me there to die. I whistled through the house in a great rage. I went in her room and screamed at her bed, at her almost empty wardrobe.

"How dare you Mother? How could you do that to your own child? Why even bats and spiders love their children and defend them with their lives. How could you? Why did you do that to me?"

Livid with indignation, I hoped, wherever she was, she could hear my ranting. I caught sight of my terrible face in the mirror and tried with all my might to send her that picture together with my rebukes of her meanness. I caught sight of her wooden trinket boxes on the dressing table and with the force of my anger sent them flying across the room. I stared at what I had just done. I turned to the mirror, yes, I was still there but growing fainter already. Surprise took my anger away and I disappeared again. I decided to use my anger. The first thing I did was to smash a window. It was one of two barred windows above the stairs that roofed the cupboard. The splintering of glass was such a satisfying sound, that I whirled around delighted by my new power. I spent the next years gathering petals, floating them through the window and holes in the wooden stairs and covering my little girl. Those petals kept their delicate scents in the dry cupboard and protected my girl and made her pretty again.

It was about this time that I began noticing the light. A new light that seemed to want me to come close. I always turned my back on it. I didn't trust light, always expected Mother's hostile being to suddenly hove into view. Besides there were other things going on, which were far more interesting. There were new noises beyond the brambles. Unseen, I observed monstrous machines with enormous wheels, men in brightly coloured caps of the strangest design in charge of giant scraping machines. They dug up the road outside the house, made it bigger and later they covered it in black, sticky stuff that stank. When they had finished, I went and had a look and was impressed by the smoothness. Many more machines drove passed the house on the new road. They were all the colours of the rainbow. I liked watching them and catching glimpses of the people inside.

14

One summer day two men came into the front garden. They cut back the brambles to the front door. One of the men had a lot of keys. He tried several and found the right one to unlock the door and they came in. It was so strange to hear voices in the house. Their arms were showing. One of them had blonde hair, he wasn't very tall but he was a big man. I observed him closely. Not Father, not Marcel, but there was a likeness. He and the other man looked around the house then they went back out and locked up the big front door.

"Just get what you can for it," said the one. His voice was like Father's but softer, then they went away again. Not long after, a silver machine crunched over the brambles in the front. A different fair-haired man got out. You could see his bare arms and his legs sticking out of his clothes. A lady got out of the other side. She wore such clothes too and her skin was so dark brown, it was almost black. I was reminded of the book in Father's study and was fascinated. She had black curls, cut short to her head and brown eyes with long lashes and there were jewels in the lobes of her ears that sparkled in the sun. She was very sleek and very beautiful. I couldn't stop staring at her and followed as they wandered around my house. They were holding hands at first then they were swiping through cobwebs protesting loudly. Such a lot of fuss – it was only a few old cobwebs.

They ended up in the kitchen. The lady leant against the dusty table, watching the man as he paced in front of her. The man's eyes were glowing. The lady looked full of doubt.

"I know it's a lot of work," the man said, "but it's going to make a wonderful home and we can make such a beautiful garden for Celeste."

The lady was looking at the brambles scrambling to come in the window. One tendril had found its way in and her eyes followed its progress along the floor. She pursed her lips.

"Well, it certainly does need a lot of work." She stood up crossing her arms, shaking her head.

He put his hands on her waist and looked into her eyes with great earnestness.

"I promise you, Simone, I can make this a wonderful home for us."

She looked away from him and at the brambles again. She sighed and shook her head. Then looked back into his eyes.

"You better, Bruno Fournier," she said, "You just better make this into a lovely home for me and our daughter!"

He beamed and put his arms around her. She smiled back, but it looked as if she wasn't quite sure she really wanted to and she was still shaking her head. Then he kissed her on the lips. They smiled at and kissed each other a lot. I didn't know where to look. Then he stepped back and pulling at her hands said,

"That's settled then, come on let's go and tell the estate agent before he sells it to someone else."

He released one of her hands and she let him pull her to the front door,

"I really don't think you need to worry about that Bruno," she was saying as they went.

15

Alone again, I fretted about what this would mean for me. This was my house. What about me and the bats and my little girl in her cupboard? I wondered who Celeste might be. Would she be horrible like Mother? I flitted about in a state of agitation, but nothing happened for days and nights, so I forgot about Bruno and Simone. The nights were warm, the moon bright, so I flew with the bats by night and collected fresh petals for the girl by day. Then Bruno came back. Big machines rolled over the front brambles. More cars came. Bruno showed the men around, some wrote on boards and tapped on small machines, which flashed and buzzed and made funny little tunes. Dates were agreed, two weeks, three weeks, six weeks.

Bruno and Simone came. Their arms and legs were covered this time. Simone wore blue breeches, of a sort, that went down to her ankles, but her toes showed through her shoes. Her toenails were bright pink and very shiny. They went through all the rooms, sticking coloured squares of paper on the furnishings. A few days later men came and put the pink papered objects in their machine and drove them away. The rest of the furniture was moved together and covered in sheets. I went from room to room in a state of great consternation.

The day after, pandemonium began. So many people, so much noise. Holes were made in walls and floors were taken up. They cleared the pantry right away. The wall between Alice and Marie's room and the store was smashed down. It's pieces sent out through the window and chained yellow buckets to a metal bin waiting below. Who to protect, bats or girl? Girl. I became her sentry, ready to attack anyone who came near but no one did. Thankfully towards evening, the men all left. Silence rang and I drifted around, appalled by the mess. In a fury, I shook the chains of the yellow bins but my rage was impotent.

The attic remained unchanged. My little friends were doggedly huddled in the darkest corners. The invasion continued day after day. Men whistled all around, thumping, bad singing, shouts and bellows of laughter. I wrapped my arms around my head and hung on. The terrible noises ceased. There were other new noises but quieter, humming and murmurings, the voices of Simone and Bruno but I didn't like them anymore. I heard the excited voice of a little girl. I swung on my perch, feeling mean and spiteful. That other light that always followed me became an insistent nuisance. I snarled at it to get away and leave me alone. My voice was harsh and bitter like Mother's and I felt pleased. I intended to hang in morose hostility forever. Then I heard the clock strike three and I just had to go out and have a look.

16

In the corridor, the tiles were back in place but the walls had changed from the dull green of old to bright white and there were pictures all along. The kitchen walls were the colour of primrose petals and there were pale wood cupboards all around. Our old table was back in place and I was cheered to see my little table and chair too. My table was covered in brightly daubed pictures, with a tray of coloured circles and little brushes in a pot of water.

The dining room was fresh and bright, our furniture back in place and the clock's pendulum swinging its old rhythm. Everything looked polished and cared for. The day room was now lined with books including I was pleased to note my father's and on another shelf Marcel's. Across the corridor, the carpeted parlour had a big white board with lined drawings. I could hear the family in the chapel so I slipped in there and stared around at the transformation. Gone were the dusty benches and tall table. All was light and clean. Simone and Bruno were reclining on comfortable couches. There were more pictures and tall plants and beautiful music was quietly playing all around.

A little girl on tiptoe was gazing out of the glass windows of the door leading out to the back garden. Her hair was a mass of golden ringlets, lit up by the sun. She was bobbing up and down, "Squirrels," she said, "Oh! Squirrels gone up the tree." She laughed in delight and turned around. Her big, blue eyes widened in surprise and then crinkled as she smiled in new delight. She was all sparkles and dimples and pretty, white teeth surrounded by her golden hair.

"Oh! Hello!"

She was looking at me. I realised that she could see me. How could this be? I wasn't even angry. I wasn't even trying. Bruno and Simone were smiling at her.

"Who are you saying hello to Celeste?" they asked.

She bobbed up and down making her ringlets dance, "Girl there, girl there."

She pointed a chubby finger right at me. I flashed through the wall.

"Gone! Girl gone!" I heard her call in surprise.

I went back to my girl. My poor, pale skinned, unloved, dead girl and I felt my heart turn vicious as the bitter bile of injustice welled up inside me.

During the night, I explored the rest of the house. It was a moonless night but darkness is my friend. I could turn on their flashy new lights just by thinking about it. I found Simone and Bruno's bedroom. They were in a huge bed, fast asleep, so I flicked the light on and off, on, off, on, off, till they awoke. I smirked at their bewilderment. I left them and the lights went off. I went to find their beloved Celeste. She slept up in the room that had been two, and where once Alice and Marie had slept. There was a glowing cat light on the chest of drawers next to her bed. By the light of the cat, I watched her sleeping face. Little puffs of air were blowing in and out and every now and then her eyebrows crinkled as if she was dreaming. I looked away and noticed all the toys. She had so many. I looked at each of them in turn. Some surprised me with their flashing lights, some talked and made music, loud in the night. Celeste didn't wake up. Simone did though and came up to check on her daughter. She looked from the peacefully sleeping face and frowned around the room at the silent, static toys. She was still frowning as she started down the stairs. I turned off the light and smirked again as she cursed and felt her way down.

The next day, I was satisfied to hear Bruno having an argument with the man I now knew to be the electrician. He and Simone were tetchy and only had smiles for Celeste. I watched her while she was busy painting at my table. She was so happy and pretty, I could see why they loved her so much. The rest of the time, I followed her from a distance. I didn't want her to see me. Despite having all those toys in her room, she spent nearly all her time downstairs with Simone. Simone had a special room where she sewed. She had a machine that whirred and made beautiful clothes for Celeste. Too many for one girl. She tied labels on the surplus garments and packed them up to be sent away to other children.

I played with the toys in Celeste's room. I especially liked the little people in the miniature house. There was a little boy in a sailor suit and a little girl and parents and Alice and the gardener but no Marie. There was a little dog and a cat and a lot of furniture in different rooms. There was no cane but sometimes the girl whacked the mother with an umbrella. Sometimes she whacked everyone even Alice and the dog and cat. She locked Marcel in the cupboard and the mother in the oven. I spent hours in that house. But it still wasn't enough. Someone needed to be punished. Celeste might be innocent but so I had been. I retired to my cupboard and plotted her punishment.

17

It was easy. I had all I needed inside my head. The next night, I returned to Celeste's room. While she was drifting into sleep, I spoke to her in harsh whispers.

"You're going to be locked in the cupboard," I began, "It's dark in there and bats will claw your hair and spiders run across your face. You can't get out. Ever. You're going to die in there."

In this way, I fed images of my life into her dreams. It had the desired effect. She awoke screaming and sobbing as I had done so many times. I hid myself from her when Simone and Bruno came charging in to comfort her. They soothed and rocked her, trying to allay her fears. Night after night, I got my revenge and watched them become irritated and irrational after another night of incoherent sobbing. No wonder Mother had been so consistently mean to me. It felt so powerful. During the days, Simone spent time with Celeste in her bedroom, trying to help Celeste feel happier there. They sat on the floor playing together. I peered at them from behind a curtain.

"Lets visit the House People" Simone suggested. She tapped on the front door of the house. "Hello," she called, opening the front wall of the house up. "Anybody home?"

Celeste remained engrossed with taking out and replacing parts of a wooden picture on the floor.

Simone gave a little gasp and retrieved the mother from where she was sticking out of the oven. She turned to her daughter. "Celeste," she asked quietly. "Why did you put the mummy in the cooker?"

Celeste turned innocent blue eyes towards her then went back to what she was doing. Simone studied her for a moment then turned back to the house. She quietly picked up the girl from where she was standing over the Alice and unclipped the umbrella from her hand. She put the Alice in a rocking chair. Silently she changed things around, raising her eyebrows when she discovered Marcel in the cupboard. She decided to put all the family on chairs around the kitchen table. That night I changed everything back again. How I smirked the next time she looked in. She couldn't believe her eyes.

Simone took Celeste to see a doctor about her 'night terrors'. Later, she talked about what the doctor had said with Bruno. It was the first time they had spoken for days. They looked very different from the happy couple who had first come to the house. No more kisses or smiles. They had dark rings under their eyes and Simone's hair had grown into a frazzle she couldn't be bothered to care about. I knew Bruno was struggling to work and his formerly cheerful screen calls were terse and less frequent. Simone told Bruno, that she hated it here and wanted to sell the house. They had an argument, trying to be quiet for the sake of their daughter but she knew and tears rolled into the turned down corners of her mouth. I returned to the cupboard. Feeling miserable, I felt around for what was left of little Rose and thought about Alice and Marie. What would they be thinking of me now? The little girl under her mound of petals had been kind. Not a witch. I wanted to slip back inside her bones and lie peacefully forever but I couldn't. I asked myself why I was terrifying Celeste when I knew so well how that felt. And why was I trying to be like Mother? Mother was horrible. My shame condensed my resentment into a bitter hard-boiled nut. I would have liked to retch and sick it out but I couldn't. I left Celeste alone at night now, but the night terrors didn't.

The light, which had seemed absent recently, returned brighter than ever. I tutted and turned away. I needed to think about how to make amends.

18

That night I sat by Celeste and told her about the nice things as I had done with the little dying girl, all those years ago. I had thought she was asleep but then realised that she had opened her eyes and was watching me. I stopped talking.

"Are you alright?" she whispered.

She looked worried about me! I nodded, shame faced. "Good," she said.

She gazed into my eyes a moment then solemnly whispered, "Do you want to be my friend?"

I nodded and she smiled at me and I smiled back.

"What's your name?"

"Grace."

Her blue eyes widened and shone in the glow.

"Grace! That's a pretty name."

My heart warmed up. She sat up and turned on the big light. The blue eyes turned questioning, "Would you like me to tell you a story?"

I nodded again and she bounced out of bed and found two books from the ones on her shelf. She clambered back in and patted the bed beside her. "Come by me, there's plenty of room."

I drifted beside her. Feeling her warmth, I was worried.

"Am I making you cold?"

She shook her head. "No, it's very hot in here. Do you find?" She kicked at the cloudy quilt above her legs and we giggled. Then she told me the stories and showed me her favourite pictures and asked me which ones were mine. After a while she leaned back against her pillow. She was still talking but her eyes kept closing and then mid-sentence she fell asleep. I stayed in the warmth of my new friend, feeling blessed by two wonderful discoveries. The first was that I had been given another chance. The second, was that, all those years ago, my mother had looked down on me, her baby daughter and loved me enough to call me Grace, which is a pretty name.

19

Waking up on their different edges of bed, Simone and Bruno asked each other if they had heard Celeste during the night. Simone rushed up and peered at her daughter, who was still fast asleep. Relieved and feeling more refreshed than she had for a long time, Simone went down to share the good news and some breakfast with Bruno. Now that she had a playmate, Celeste spent much more time in her bedroom. We didn't really bother with the toys that much, preferring our own made-up games. She adored laughing. I loved laughing with her and we could return to the same silliness time and again, hysteria mounting until she could hardly breathe. I liked listening to her talking with her parents and how they would accept whatever she had to say with amused tolerance.

"Who were you talking to upstairs?" Bruno might ask.

"Grace." She would reply, nonchalantly spooning in more of whatever dinner was that day.

At first, I was made anxious by her openness, fearing swift retribution for her or me, but this was a different family and with time I stopped being watchful for repercussions. It amused Celeste hugely that only she could see me and she would often share conspiratorial giggles and whispers with me at the table. Her parents, so pleased to see her happy again played along with her imaginary friend. A place was always set for me at the table and sometimes Simone would ask what Gracie might like for dinner today.

"I've told you Mummy, it's Grace not Gracie." Celeste would reprimand and Simone would apologise and she and Bruno would exchange their own secret smiles. Simone looked sleek and Bruno could concentrate on his work again so warmth was resumed to their relations. I loved being part of this family and felt even more empowered by my ability to change things for the better than when I had been changing them for the worse.

One summers day, when Celeste and I were arranging a toys' tea party under the lilac roses, I became aware that the bolt of the cupboard door was being hammered. I flashed through and used all the power I could muster to prevent Simone from succeeding in hammering it out. Celeste ran in and took in a shocked breath of air when she saw what Simone was doing.

"Stop Mummy, Stop!" She shouted, grabbing and pulling at her clothes.

Simone turned round in surprise. "But why Honey?"

"Because that's Grace's cupboard."

"Well, can't we ask Grace if I can take a look in there?"

Celeste was crying, "No Mummy, no we mustn't."

Simone knelt down in front of Celeste, "But why not Little One?" she asked gently. "It might be Grace's cupboard but it's in my house and I only want to look."

Celeste was shaking her head, "You're not allowed to look in there."

"But why not?"

Celeste moved her tear-stained face close to Simone's and whispered. "Because that's where she keeps her bones."

Simone's eyes widened. She stared at Celeste for a moment then gathered her silently crying daughter in her arms and rocked her gently to comfort her. "There, there," she murmured, "Mummy's not, nobody's going in the cupboard, there, there."

While Celeste was sleeping later that evening, I eavesdropped on the adults' conversation about what had taken place.

"Well, I don't believe in that sort of thing either Bruno," Simone was saying, "But clearly, she does."

Unusually, they were having a drink of something that smelt strong in glasses that rang with cubes of ice.

"Ok, ok, well," he sniffed and sipped the drink and gave his glass a little swirl, "Well, I suppose we don't really need that cupboard. If it upsets her, let's just leave it shut. I'm sure she'll grow out of it one day."

Simone took a little sip and nodded at him over the rim of her glass. The next day she quietly added a padlock to prevent the bolt from opening fully. My girl was going to stay safe under her rose petals.

20

Simone began talking to Celeste about school. I couldn't believe it. Remembering the sudden and permanent disappearance of Marcel, I was seized by panic and begged Celeste not to go.

"Now, you tell me, why you don't want to go to school." Simone asked after listening to Celeste's adamant insistence that she wouldn't be going.

"I don't want to go, because I can't leave Grace here on her own and I'll miss you too Mummy."

"Hmm well, you know, school only lasts for a tiny bit of the day." Simone said looking directly at us. She stood up, turned and began walking around the room, talking, loud and clearly.

"Hello Grace!" she began, looking in the opposite direction.

Celeste and I exchanged grins. "I know you love Celeste as much as I do. Now, it's time for Celeste to go to school so she can learn lots of things that are important for her to know. Now, I know that you will want her to do well at school so she can achieve her full potential. Thank you, Grace."

She sat down again in front of us.

"Mummy," said Celeste, her voice brimming over with laughter, "Grace is sitting right here next to me."

"Well," Simone smiled at us leaning forward on her elbows, "That's alright then."

Celeste started school a few days later. I missed her but it was different to Marcel. What Simone had said was true, Celeste was only gone a few hours of the day. When she got home, she told us about her day and I learned to read and how to do arithmetic with her. Over time her reading books changed from simple stories with cute pictures to information books. I found these very interesting and learnt so many things about this clever, modern world, in which I now found myself. One morning while Celeste was at school and Bruno was out on a site meeting, a man in a black robe came to the house. Simone invited him in and they stood outside the cupboard door. Simone looked troubled and I watched anxiously from above.

"In here, you say?" the man asked.

"Yes, but I'm not opening it. I can't, I've promised."

I hadn't seen Simone in such a state for a long time.

"That's fine, that's fine, no problem at all." The man had a soothing voice and seemed kind. "I'll just prepare myself if you don't mind. Perhaps I could use another room?"

"Of course." Simone opened the door to the dining room. "Will this be alright?"

"Oh yes, this'll be fine. I'll only be a minute."

She closed the door and he took a white tunic out of his bag and put it on. Then he placed a silky, purple stole around his neck. He took a cross with a man on it and placed it on the dining room table. I was reminded of my father's book. I had seen this suffering man, nailed by hands and feet to the terrible cross before. The robed man put his hands together under his chin and muttered a few words. Outside in the corridor Simone seemed to be having an argument with herself. She jumped when the man opened the door.

"All set," he said.

I watched him closely, as did Simone. He held up the cross towards the cupboard door and spoke in a clear, calm voice, "Demons, I command you to retreat!"

Simone stepped forward. "Oh no, she's not a demon. She's just a dead, little girl. She seems like a really nice child."

The man opened his eyes. "Oh, don't worry about that," he told her. "It's just what we say." He closed his eyes again. "Now young Grace, it's time for you to relinquish this world and answer the call of Our Father. He loves you and wants you to be by his side. When our time comes we will all follow you to be with Him."

He opened his eyes and smiled at the door. Then he spoke a few words to Our Father and Hail Mary.

The man finished speaking and turned to face Simone.

"Is that it?" she asked.

"Yes, no flashes of brimstone, I'm afraid."

He smiled at her and she tried to smile back but it didn't quite happen.

He patted her arm. "It'll be fine," he said then nodding toward the dining room door, "I'll just go and change."

When he came back out, Simone handed him an envelope, "Thank you." she said. "Here, please, it's a donation for, you know, good things."

He thanked her and told her again not to worry and that everything was going to be fine. When she'd seen him out, she walked quickly back to the cupboard door, hands pressed over mouth. "I'm so sorry Grace. I was only trying to help. I'm so sorry." She slid down against the door. "What have I done?" she sobbed. "What have I done?"

I was unscathed by the incident because I am not a witch and sought to reassure her. I concentrated hard and was able to tinkle Rose's bell a few times. Simone heard it and stopped crying. She stared ahead, disbelieving of her ears. I tinkled it again. Simone smiled through her tears.

"Thank you, Grace," she called. "Thank you, dear, sweet Grace. I promise I will never do anything like that again." She wiped her face with her hands and got up. She was weepy for the rest of the morning but had pulled herself together by the time the others came home. She never told them about that morning. We kept it to ourselves.

21

When Celeste was ten, Simone and Bruno started talking about a new school. They showed her some brochures and told her that she could choose to go to the school nearby or to a school that had better facilities but was further away, which meant she would have to stay there during term time. I couldn't look at her. She considered for a moment but told them she wanted to choose the school near home. There were three sighs of relief.

Time seemed to go faster now. There were often friends in Celeste's room. They did each other's hair and make-up, gossiped, sang and danced. Mostly they laughed, occasionally someone was crying. I watched them, learning from them all the time. One afternoon during the long summer holidays of her sixteenth year, Celeste was reading in a hammock. I was up one of the trees to which it was attached, just feeling dreamy. Celeste suddenly sat up and turned. She put the novel she had been reading on the grass next to her feet and took off her sunglasses.

"You know Grace," she said, "I don't think the man you thought of as your father was your father."

I raised my eyebrows and moved close to her.

Her next announcement raised my eyebrows even higher.

"I think your father was the soldier with the sparkly eyes."

She told me about the book she had been reading, a historical romance. The story was set in the nineteenth century and told of a young girl who fell in love with a soldier. He had to go to war but shortly after he left, she discovered that he had made her pregnant. To avoid bringing shame on the family, it was agreed that the girl, Marie-Cecile, would marry a bachelor friend of the family. A man much older than she was. Letters she wrote to the soldier were burned, not sent. There were conditions to the agreement. There was to be no further contact with the soldier. The illegitimate child would not be seen or heard by anyone. Marie-Cecile would behave as a true wife to her new husband and provide him with heirs. The story went on. Brave Marie-Cecile ran away before the wedding took place and after many twists and turns, she and her son were reunited with her soldier and she married the right man.

But I was no longer listening.

"Do you see what I mean though Grace?" Celeste raked her fingers through her thick blond waves. Seeing my confusion, she added more gently, "It would explain a few things, wouldn't it?"

For the first time ever, I wanted to get away from Celeste.

"I didn't mean to upset you," she called after me, "Grace, come back! I was only trying to help!"

I retreated to the dry petal darkness of the cupboard. I needed to be alone to process this information. Celeste's tale changed everything. Mother's heartlessness was explained. She had felt betrayed and entrapped. No wonder she had poured all her love into Marcel if she had been forbidden to love me.

I felt guilty about leaving Celeste and found her in her room. She was crying.

"That's why I had cursed eyes," I said.

She turned to me, her eyes puffy and spilling. She nodded, "They were just like his weren't they."

We talked my sad tale through. To dope and abandon anyone, as she had me, remained an unforgivable act but what was her choice? To remain in isolation forever with her entrapping daughter or grasp her opportunity of a life worth living with the 'fancy man' who made her laugh. What a choice!

"No one should have had to make that choice," muttered Celeste, "They wouldn't have to these days."

I thought back to Mother's brisk smiles the day that she had locked me in the cupboard for the last time. What thoughts had they been hiding? How must she have been feeling? I suddenly remembered a forgotten detail of that day. I suddenly remembered the kittens, their writhing and Father, his groaning. Mother's ministrations.

"I wonder what would have happened if I had eaten the bread," I said.

Celeste looked at me questioningly. I explained about the bread, stale and uneaten.

"You think, she meant to actually poison you?"

I nodded. "I don't think she expected me to wake up."

We looked at each other. It seemed to make more sense.

"Oh Grace! Your mother was awful to you. I don't care what her excuses were."

I smiled, grateful for my friend's heated condemnation.

"She was." I agreed. "She really was awful to me, but at least I understand why she was like that now."

I thanked Celeste for providing me with the key that unlocked my mother's secrets. I knew that we were soon to drift apart but at that moment Celeste and I had never felt closer.

22

And so it was. Celeste progressed through her final years of school. She met her first boyfriend and broke his heart. She fell head over heels for the next one and he broke hers. Celeste encountered the brutality of rejection. Bruno and Simone held her tight and soothed her tears and I helped in my way but it was her friends, her peers, as Simone called them who were her real confidants now. There was talk of college and shortly after an exuberant party in the back garden. Celeste packed her bags. She told me many times that she was going to miss me and that she wished she could take me with her but I sensed an overriding excitement for things that didn't include me. I told her I would miss her too and be thinking of her every day. The house felt empty without her. Bruno and Simone went away more too. I envied their ability to seek distraction from their sadness.

Celeste came home for the holidays and tried to describe her new life to me but it was beyond my imagination and the breaks became shorter and rarer. After college, Celeste got a job in a far away town. She would have screen chats with Simone and Bruno and describe her new life and show them around her flat. Often a young man would say hello too and on a much looked forward to visit, she brought him with her. He seemed serious and thoughtful. She wore a new ring on her finger and Martin slept with her in her room instead of me. When they were leaving, she hugged her parents and tears were shed because their new jobs would be taking them abroad. She took the time to call goodbye to me but, with a pang, I realised that, even though I was right in front of her, Celeste could no longer see me. They were just about to go when Celeste suddenly dashed to the stairs.

"I have to do this," she ran up the stairs calling out, "Grace, Grace! Meet me in my room."

I was there but she couldn't see me. She closed the door, panting.

She looked around. "Grace," she whispered urgently, "Grace, I just had to tell you, I'm pregnant Grace. I'm going to have a baby."

She was still searching for me and I desperately tried to think of a way to let her know I was there.

"You're the first person to know. I haven't even told Martin yet." Tears were springing from her eyes and tracing her cheeks. Tracing down to the first beginnings of her first wrinkles just framing the corners of her mouth. She was so happy and sad she was bursting. "If it's a girl, Grace, I'm going to name her after you. I'm going to call her Grace."

I so wanted to let her know I was pleased for her. She was standing up, wiping the tears from her face. "I have to go."

As her hand turned the handle of the door, she turned back for a last glance around the room. "I will always love you Grace."

She was going down the stairs. I rushed to the cupboard and tinkled Rose's bell but the dining room clock was chiming and she didn't hear. They were saying goodbyes again. Suddenly I knew what to do. I flashed out to the front garden and flew rose petals from the red flowered bush to make a heart shape on the windscreen of their car. There was just enough dampness in the air to make them stick. The look on Celeste's face when she saw my petal heart is a moment I will treasure for ever.

"Those weren't there a minute ago," Martin exclaimed as Celeste carefully picked the petals off the glass.

"Grace!" whispered Celeste, "I'm keeping these."

She smiled a secret smile and I knew who she would be keeping them for.

As they got in the car Celeste said to Martin, "Now do you believe me about Grace?"

"Looks like I have to."

She nodded at the vague heart printed by the petals on the windscreen as the car engine started. The car drove out of the drive and down the road and my beautiful, golden Celeste was gone.

22

Simone and Bruno began talking about downsizing. Estate agents came and took pictures. People came for viewings. Simone and Bruno started putting things in boxes and then one day a lorry pulled in and their belongings were taken away. Bruno came back in from putting more stuff in the car then he and Simone went and stood at the cupboard door. "Goodbye Grace," they called. "Goodbye, dear Grace. We hope you like your new people." They both had tears in their eyes.

They walked to the front door and I heard the big, old key lock it behind them.

The new people held no interest for me. It was a couple, Patrick and Ada, who liked to cook and had people around to share their meals frequently. They liked to drink fine wines with the different courses and became very talkative and laughed a lot. They had two little dogs, who growled whenever they sensed my presence, hackles raised, much to the bewilderment of Patrick and Ada. I retreated to my cupboard, ignoring the increased daily activity outside. Patrick and Ada were making changes. It was a shock for me one day when the cupboard door was unscrewed from its bolt and hinges and wrenched away. A portly man grunted in surprise when he saw the mound of dried petals. He stuck his head in the cupboard and sniffed then went away. He returned a few minutes later with a bin sack. With some effort, he knelt down and began shoving the petals in the sack. I flitted about but, really, it didn't seem to matter anymore and I was powerless to stop him anyway. He made a very loud grunt and jumped back when he discovered what was underneath. With another grunt he heaved himself up and trotted off in search of Patrick and Ada. The three of them came and Patrick and Ada stood over my bones in stunned silence.

"I'll call the police." said Ada.

The workman stood in front of her. He nodded towards inside the cupboard, cleared his throat and spoke in a low voice.

"It's a sad thing to find," he began.

Ada and Patrick nodded, hopeful of any guidance in this matter.

"It's up to you," he said. "But if you call the police, they're going to take up all of this floor and probably," he nodded towards the east, west corridor, "That floor as well. It could be years before you get this place straight again."

Patrick and Ada blinked at him. Ada gave a little twitch.

"So, what are you suggesting?" Patrick looked uncomfortable and perplexed.

"If it was me," the man nodded at the cupboard again, "The colour of those bones? They've been in there for years. Why do you think that padlock was on the door? The previous owners had a look, saw what was in there, locked it up again."

He shook his head at this neglect of duty.

"If it was me," he began again, "I'd dig a hole," his head nodded toward the back garden, "Bury that and put a nice bush on top. Rest assured; I won't say anything."

Patrick and Ada stared at him in utter incredulity.

"It'd have to be quite deep," he added, "On account of the dogs."

He watched the eyebrows of his employers shoot up even higher.

"It's up to you," he said. "I'm going to go now. I'll come back in the morning and carry on unless I hear from you."

He pursed his lips and shook his head, "Because, if you do decide to call the police, you won't be needing me again for a long time."

He knelt down, put his tools in his bag and stood back up.

"Of course, if I were to find more of the same, then would be the time to call the police. In my opinion."

He picked up his bag. "I'll be off then."

Ada and Patrick went into the kitchen and had a hushed debate about how to deal with my bones. After about twenty minutes the debate came to a conclusion and the decision was made. They went and walked around the back garden to choose my spot. Eventually the right position was agreed on. It was quite far down, where the vegetable garden would have been but was now a flat, green lawn.

"Right, well you'd better get a move on Ada." Patrick told her. "They're going to close in about half an hour aren't they?"

Ada went dashing off to the garden centre and Patrick fetched his spade and began digging. The dogs ran around the garden, excited by this sudden burst of activity. Ada took ages. When she came back Patrick was sweating profusely and up to his chest in the hole. He'd thrown his shirt off, which was lying in a sweaty ball next to the surrounding heap of earth.

"Good grief!" Ada cried. "Well done! That ought to be deep enough."

"It's supposed to be deeper than this," he said and carried on. "Trouble is, the deeper I go the harder it gets. We could do with a digger for this sort of job."

"Well, we're not getting one of those." Ada peered down at him. "Besides, surely that's deep enough. I mean you know," she looked around and lowered her voice. "It's not smelly. The smells have all gone. And we are putting the rose bush on top. I got a lovely one. It's pure white, which signifies innocence and is most appropriate for the death of a young person." She watched his stoically digging torso.

"It's called Lune, which is French for the moon and has a delightful scent of gardenia and old-fashioned tea rose."

Patrick leant on his spade, looking up at her.

"Yes, I think this'll do," he said. "Now to get out."

With Ada's help, he managed to scramble out and leant on his spade again, surveying his task and puffing.

"That'll have to do."

Ada scooped up his shirt. "I'll bring you a drink," she called disappearing into the house. She came out a minute later with a large glass of water, a towel and a fresh shirt, which she thought would be more appropriate for 'the next part'.

Patrick gulped down the water, towelled himself down and got the shirt on.

"Right!" he said, "Next part." and followed Ada into the house. I followed too. I wasn't at all distressed as once I would have been. I appreciated their soul-searching over my remains and felt relieved they had decided to keep me and move me to a more permanent place in the garden I loved.

There was conjecture about 'the next part'. In addition to the rose, Ada had bought a rather beautiful cream shawl, to wrap me in.

"Look, we can carry it out in that, but we can't bury it in it."

"Why not? We can't just put it in the mud Patrick. That's just horrible." Ada was close to tears.

"I know, I know, but it's modern isn't it. If it did get dug up, they'd trace it back to us, wouldn't they."

Ada hadn't thought of that. "God! Yes you're right!" She hung the shawl on the banister. "Let me get some rubber gloves, we don't want our DNA all over it do we."

While she was gone, Patrick laid out the shawl on the floor next to the cupboard door. He considered how to manœuvre the skeleton on to it. Only the legs showed through the door, the rest was behind the wooden panelling of the front of the cupboard. He was trying unsuccessfully to pull the panelling away, when Ada returned.

"They knew what they were doing in those days," he told her, "I can't get this to budge an inch."

I knew what Patrick meant.

He gave up. "I'll just have to try to get it out in one piece like this."

Ada was looking at his muddy shoes on the shawl.

"Sorry!" he said and removed himself.

She handed him the gloves. "It looks like a one-man job, I'm afraid."

"Yes."

He pulled on the gloves and knelt down. Ever so carefully he pulled and twisted the skeleton out and on to the shawl. Ada watched making encouraging noises. There were a few breakages.

"Oh sorry, I'm so sorry." He kept saying, laying the next bits gently down and Ada would wince in sympathy.

Once he'd got all the bones out. He stood up with a great, shuddering sigh.

"I know what to do," said Ada. She showed him the bin sack full of dry petals. "We'll put a bed of these down. Then we'll put another layer on top. Somebody went to a lot of trouble to collect all these. I think we should re-use them."

Patrick nodded. "Good idea. Right next phase. Wait, I'm going to get a ladder."

He set the ladder in the hole. Ada brought out the sack of petals and they poured enough in to cover the base. They carefully carried the shawl and its contents to the burial plot and with Patrick climbing down the ladder, step by step, lowered the shawl respectfully in. They both gave a relieved sigh then Patrick lovingly moved the shawl from under the bones and arranged them as he thought best.

"There." Patrick stood up, handed the shawl to Ada and climbed out.

"Do you think we should say a prayer or something?" asked Ada.

Patrick looked down at the bones on their bed of crispy petals. "Rest In Peace, Little One."

"Yes, Rest In Peace," chimed Ada.

She began pouring the rest of the petals in. As she did so there was a little tinkling sound as Rose's bell fell in amongst them.

"Right!" said Patrick and began piling in the earth. Ada fetched the rose bush.

It was almost dark by the time they had finished and the rose had been watered in.

The blooms shone out in the darkness.

"Lune!" said Ada.

"Good choice." said Patrick. "Now come on. Let's crack open a bottle of the white Bordeaux. I think we deserve it."

23

The cupboard is gone. The attic is where I pass my time now. At night I fly around with the bats. The scent of the lune rose fills the air and its glowing blooms attract the nectar seekers. Summer is fading and soon the bats will be staying in. The 'calling light' still follows me. It's as reassuring to me now as Rose's bell once was. I'm thinking of going towards it and allowing myself to be engulfed in its glow. It seems to me that I have learned all there is to learn from this long and strange existence. The golden light fondly reminds me of the first time Celeste smiled at me with the sunshine framing her golden curls. I allow the light to bathe me and draw me in.

Light. Enlightenment.

Red light.

I am aware. I am floating free. I move in my vessel of red warmth. I am soothed by the shushing and regular beating. I swallow and inhale what is around me. If I like, I smile, if not I frown. This is familiar. Voices and laughter and calm. The red goes brighter, the red goes dull. I like to push against the walls. Sensations of contact that react to my pushes.

I fill my space. I have to turn around. It's difficult. I don't like difficult. I can no longer swim or push. The shushing and beating reach a crescendo. There are changes and I am being squeezed, squeezed smaller and tighter. All the fluid in my lungs is squeezed out.

Light, bright lights. Loud din. I blink around. I know things.

I recognise. Celeste is smiling down at me. Such devotion.

"Hello little one," she smiles, "Hello my little Grace,"

"Look! She's smiling," says another so softly. Martin.

"That'll be wind, not a proper smile," a different voice, cheerful, authoritative, not one of mine.

In turn I gaze at Celeste and Martin. They gaze at me.

I must remember, I must remember all that I know.

Another face looms close. Almost black eyes twinkle into mine.

"Look Grace," Celeste takes in us both, "This is Jean-Vincent,"

"Hello Grace," Jean-Vincent whispers and plants a careful kiss on my brow.

"I'm your big brother," he tells me solemnly, "And I'm going to look after you always."

I stare in turn at my family.

I am full and warm and comfortable. My eyes close. While I sleep the past passes. When I awaken my clarity of vision is reduced. All that I want is to feed. I must adjust to this milk passing through me, this gravity, the soft but hard that doesn't allow free movement. I like to be held so I can hear the regular beat that lulls me. I am newborn. Apart from occasional flashes and dreams, all that I knew before is gone. But this time I am lucky. This time I am loved.

Bibliography:

The Italian Comedy By Pierre Louis Duchartre

Authorized translation from French to English by Randolf T. Weaver

Printed in Great Britain
by Amazon